D0398832

FREEDOM
SWIMMER

FREEDOM
SWIMMER

WAI CHIM

SCHOLASTIC PRESS / NEW YORK

Library of Congress Cataloging-in-Publication Data Available

ISBN 978-1-338-65613-8

1 2021

Printed in the U.S.A.   23

First US edition, October 2021
Book design by Baily Crawford

For my father

A note about phonetics

I had a hard time standardizing pronunciation and phoneticizing Chinese words and idioms due to the differences in dialects and colloquialisms throughout China. (I mean, what can you do when Chairman Mao is referred to as both Mao Zedong and Mao Tse-tung in modern literature?)

As such, proper names and places generally use standard Mandarin Pinyin for ease of identification in names such as Guangzhou, Dapeng, and Ping Chau. The spellings of nicknames and everyday words in the regional dialect, especially exclamations, have mostly been chosen at my discretion.

PROLOGUE

Dapeng Peninsula, Longgang, Guangdong

Ma is gone. I fought back tears, gripping the handle of the wheelbarrow tighter so her body wouldn't tip out too soon. I was taking her to the river to join the other villagers who had passed. I didn't dare look around—what if one of those bodies had surfaced, caught on a rock instead of being swept away by the current after the last rains? I could almost picture the head of some weeks-dead villager bobbing up beside me, all sunken cheeks and lifeless eyes behind paper-thin lids.

I was surprised that even at the end, Ma's face looked plump and her cheeks soft. Her belly was swollen, but the rest of her body was all shriveled skin and knobby bones. She seemed peaceful in death, so different from her constant bitterness when she had been alive and starving.

We arrived at the riverbank, both our clothes sodden from the rain. My hands kept slipping as I tried to tip my load out of the wheelbarrow. I'd found it beside one of the many barren fields along the path, likely used for this very purpose and then abandoned. Finally, I heaved it to the side and took a few moments to arrange Ma's hands on her chest so it looked like she was sleeping, even amid the stench of rot and decay. She would stay here until the tide came in and the river carried her out to sea.

Ma's last moments had been fitful. She had been in bed for more than a week, unable to even lift her head to take a sip of water. I had tried spooning it into her mouth, but it had dribbled down the side of her face. She'd been too frail even to swallow. It was unlike her; she was usually all angry energy, like a monsoon. I had expected her last breaths to be big, powerful, that Ma would be loud and forceful even in her passing.

That was three days ago.

I'd known I had to take Ma's body to the river, but I couldn't bring myself to do it. It meant pushing the loaded wheelbarrow down to the riverbank on my own, because no one in the village was strong enough or willing to help me. Or maybe it was because it felt too final. If I took her to the river, it meant she would never again get up and make thin congee for breakfast. That she would never again sift through our meager rice flour rations to pick out the worms. Never again shout my name in a fit of rage as she chased me out of the house, feather duster raised high above her head, ready to give me a lashing.

So Ma's body had stayed on the bed, her head turned to one side like she was just resting. The first night, I kept thinking she would cough again, that she would come back to me in a wheezing, hacking fit.

My hands continued to slip as I pushed the wheelbarrow back up the muddy bank, leaving Ma's body behind. I struggled to dislodge the stuck wheel, throwing all my weight behind it. At eleven, I was small for my age, having hit my growth spurt just as the famine was taking hold. For three years, it had seemed like my body was trapped in its own prison. I was always hungry, my stomach grinding itself raw. I hadn't dared complain to Ma or Ba. We were all starving. Everyone in the village was. Ma did her best to make meals out of anything she could find. While I foraged for mollusks and snatched at tiny minnows along the shore, she cooked wild plants and even the bark and roots from nearby trees.

The villagers had grumbled under their breaths when the Cadre made the official Party announcement: "The cause of our nation's suffering has been . . . Three Years of Natural Disasters." The Cadre was the official head of our village, placed there by the Communist Party to execute the orders of Chairman Mao Zedong. A few years ago, the entire village was talking about "the Great Leap Forward," delivering glory to China. Now the Cadre had a new term for the lack of food, the hunger, the starving, and finally the dying. Like everything else, the Party had a name for it.

Three Years of Natural Disasters.

With a spurt, the wheel finally sprang free, dragging me onto the road with it. I gritted my teeth and hoisted up the handles, pointing the wheelbarrow back toward the village. The rain pattered against the steel bed. It reminded me of the small drum Ba had given me for Chinese New Year when I was three. Instead of spinning it, I'd bashed the face against the ground, clutching the thin red handle in my pudgy fists as I giggled with glee.

Now I clenched my skeletal hands around the handles of the wheelbarrow. Salty sweat mingled with the dribbles of rain, and I licked my lips. All was silent except for the rhythm of the rain and the roar of the river. Nightfall wasn't far off, and I shuddered, thinking of the packs of wild dogs that might come for Ma's body before the river rose high enough to take it. But then I remembered—the wild dogs had been hunted by the villagers for meat. The nights were silent now.

My bottom lip stung, and I realized I was biting down on it. A loud sob escaped, and then another, the salt from my tears stinging my cheeks, already tender from too much crying. I leaned into the wheelbarrow and kept walking, the rushing water drowning out my whimpers.

★ ★ ★

It had been two weeks since I'd been down to the river. I'd had nothing to eat but some bits of dried moss I'd gathered from the rocks along the banks. The rain had subsided, but the air in the village was still heavy with the stench of death. I had hardly left the house since I'd dealt with Ma's body. There was no food, no firewood, and the water in the jug was murky, with little tendrils of mosquito larvae under the woven cover. Funny how a parasite that fed on blood still sought new breeding ground when everything around it was dying.

I dropped the cover back over the jug and crawled under the netting of the wooden frame that served as our bed. There was no point in getting fresh water. I wasn't even crying anymore.

During the last two weeks, a few of the neighbors had stopped by to peek inside, and I'd hidden each time. Their curiosity wasn't new to me. Instead of being among the knot of forty or so homes that made up the rest of the village, Ba had chosen to build our house on the other side of the main road, closer to the beach. He'd said he loved waking to the gentle crashing of waves rather than the chattering of neighbors. Our house was just a hundred yards away from the others, but it was enough to arouse suspicion. Even before Ba had died, the villagers were forever peering in, and our little home was often the subject of gossip. *Reactionaries, counterrevolutionists, what's the Ming family up to?* My young ears had picked up every whisper. In a tiny village like ours, where we had nothing but one another for entertainment, choosing to be away from the group simply wasn't done.

Ba had chuckled and dismissed the whispers, but they had always bothered Ma, and they only got worse after he was gone. In some ways, the Three Years of Natural Disasters were a bit of a blessing—everyone was too desperate for themselves to mind their neighbors.

I was starting to drift off when there was a faint knock at the door. Alarmed, I held my breath and kept very still. My heart pounded. There'd been stories about orphaned children whose desperate neighbors came to pillage their meager belongings. There wasn't anything in the house worth taking, but I couldn't face the disapproving look of my father in my mind's eye if I didn't protect our home.

The knock came again, timidly. It didn't sound like one of the villagers, and no angry voice demanded to be let in. Padding over to the door, I reached for the handle.

A girl stood on the other side.

She stared, not saying a word, her hands clasped in front of her muddy clothes. Everyone in the village wore the same faded blue shirts and trousers, all cut from the same cloth our monthly rations bought. Hers were oversized and misshapen, like they might have once belonged to her elder brother. I didn't recognize her, so she couldn't have been from our village, but she must have lived close by.

"Are you by yourself?" she asked. "Is there anyone else here?"

"Why?" My voice sounded like there were rocks and metal bits grinding together in my throat. I coughed to clear it, but it felt like I was choking on ash.

The girl said nothing, and I noticed the red circles around her eyes. There were streaks of dirt on her face, and her shirt was torn.

"It's just me," I said. "Do you want to come in?" I wasn't sure why I'd asked. I had nothing to offer.

She gave a slight nod, and I stepped aside to let her through. She was cautious and careful, like a nervous wild animal. I wanted to put out a hand to calm her but kept them by my sides, especially when I saw angry gashes on her arm, like fingernail marks. Whoever she was running away from had tried hard to catch her.

She decided it was safe and moved inside.

There was a lone stool and a dusty table against the wall, but the girl ignored them and shuffled over to the stove in the corner of the room that we called a kitchen. She crouched in front of the pile of cold ashes. I hadn't bothered to light a fire in weeks, since there was nothing to hang over it.

I shifted my weight uneasily. What was she doing here? She looked as starved as me, but I didn't think she was going to rob me blind.

I tried to remember what Ma had done once upon a time, when we used to have visitors.

"Would you like some tea?" I said automatically, then frowned. "I mean, there's no tea. But I could get you some water or something."

The girl lifted the cover off the water jug to peek at the contents.

"I, ah, don't have water, really, either," I said sheepishly. "But I can get some."

She shrugged and covered the jug before flicking her eyes to me. There was a spark of curiosity in them, like she was sizing me up but not in a cruel way. My face was getting hot, and I looked down at the floor.

"What's your name?" I asked the dirt at my feet.

Silence.

"Fei. Lam Feiyen." It was so quiet I thought I'd imagined it. "I'm from Long-chi." The village, the largest of our subdistrict, was about half an hour's walk from my house.

"I'm Ming. Ming Hong," I said, and dared to glance up at her. She gave me a small smile, and my face burned.

"I'll go fetch some water." I seized the jug with both hands. I thought I had used up the last of my energy, but I seemed to have found a new source of strength.

"Okay." She dug into her pants pocket and pulled out a cupped hand to show me. Nestled in the center of it was a tiny, precious sweet potato.

My stomach hardened at the sight of it. Ma had cooked the last of our sweet potatoes a month ago. I remembered exactly what it had tasted like. She'd made a broth out of scraps of the skin that was so watered down it had really been nothing more than a muddy sludge. And we drank down every last drop.

"We can share some when you get back," she said solemnly. I almost dropped the water jug. She was offering a gift I knew I could never repay.

I tried to force out words of gratitude, but they were caught in the chalky dust in my throat. All I managed was a grudging, "Okay."

★ ★ ★

That night, beside the freshly lit stove, Fei shaved off precious slivers of her potato and mashed them into a thin broth. Part of me wanted to just gobble the whole thing. It was too small to plant, half the size of a normal sweet potato. But even though my stomach clenched at the thought of it, I knew we had to make it last as long as we could.

Fei spooned a little bit of broth into our bowls, and I nodded in thanks. I swallowed mine in just a few mouthfuls, barely tasting it as it slid down my throat. My body screamed for more, but I also knew that my stomach had shrunk too much to take it. Fei drank hers in dainty sips, letting the liquid swirl around her mouth before swallowing.

When I went to bed, Fei crawled in beside me and buried her face in my neck. I had never slept with anyone except Ma and Ba before. But I could tell from the easy way she snuggled into the crook of my shoulder that Fei was used to sharing a bed with siblings.

Fei's limbs wound around my body. She smelled earthy, like wet dirt with a tiny hint of sourness. It was different from Ma's scent, but comforting.

We lay perfectly still in the dark until I thought she was asleep. But then she spoke. "What happened to your parents?"

The lightness of her voice surprised me. No one had ever asked me something like this before—I had only ever heard sinister whispers. It took a moment for me to answer. "I took Ma to the river two weeks ago."

"And your father?"

I pressed my lips together and sighed into the silence. She pushed her fingers into my shoulder, massaging the tension from it as if she could squeeze the words out.

"My father died too. He . . . he drowned," I said in a hurried breath. I had never spoken those words before. The day he'd disappeared, Ma had forbidden me from mentioning him in her presence ever again.

"Was he a fisherman?" Fei rubbed my shoulder in gentle soothing motions. It made me miss Ma even more.

"He . . . he was swimming." A lump caught in my throat. "He went swimming at night." I didn't mention that the patrol guards had probably shot him in the dark as he tried to escape. I hadn't seen his body, but I'd heard the whispers.

Fei seemed to understand. "I'm sorry." She snuggled in closer, the points of her bones jabbing into my sides.

"What about your parents?" I asked.

She was quiet, and I felt her heart beat faster. I swallowed and pulled her in tight, her small body trembling as she tried to control her sobs.

"Ba sent my younger sister to the forest to look for berries. She never came back. Two days later, he sent me out and said if

I didn't find food, I couldn't come home." She paused, mulling over her next words. "He doesn't know I took the sweet potato," she confessed in a whisper.

We lay in silence. I thought she had fallen asleep, but then she spoke again.

"Your house is nice, so close to the ocean." Her words slurred with drowsiness. "Maybe tomorrow, we can both turn into fish and swim away."

My heart ached, and I hugged her tighter, stroking her hair. Despite its tangles, it felt as soft as the fluff of a chick.

Eventually, she fell asleep on my shoulder, and I soon followed her into slumber.

★ ★ ★

We woke in the morning to an angry knock at the door.

"Fei! I know you're in there; the villagers all saw you. Come outside this instant!" screeched a woman's voice. The mud walls shook as she pounded.

Still heavy with sleep, I nudged the girl beside me.

"Who's that?"

She didn't reply as the screech came again.

"Fei! You come out right now. You're in so much trouble, running away from home after everything we have given you. I will beat you until you fly high for your disobedience! How could you disrespect your father?"

The girl pressed her cheek against my shoulder. I started to get up and answer, but she grabbed my arm and shook her head.

"Okay, I'm coming in," the woman cried. The knocking stopped, and a more terrible silence fell over the house. Finally, Fei stood up and shuffled to the door, her small feet kicking up the dust.

She lifted the wooden bolt and opened the door just a crack, but the force outside it blew it all the way open.

"Lam Feiyen, you selfish ingrate." The woman was not much taller than Fei, but she was stout as a tree. Her hands were on her hips and her feet set wide to take up as much room as possible. Her hair was pulled up into a severe bun, and even with her tattered and patched clothes, she managed to give the appearance of being neat and trim. Fei cowered as she shouted.

"Don't think you're too old for a strong beating. I'll get a switch and beat you until you fly . . ." Her sharp eyes honed in on me. They widened in fury. I was half sitting, half lying on the wooden bed frame, my shoulders poking out of the neck of a dirty undershirt.

"Wah!" The woman walloped Fei across the ear, and she cried out in surprise. "You're shacking up with a boy! You chicken whore." Her fingers pinched Fei's earlobe, and it pulsed bright red.

"Auntie Shu!" Fei gasped as though resisting the urge to pull away in case her aunt tore her ear off. "He's my friend!"

I was paralyzed, torn between leaping up to defend her and staying put, and Fei sobbed.

"Your friend? Aiyah! How could you become friends with garbage like this? Haven't you heard about his father?" How did she know? It seemed there was no hiding from the gossip and accusations, even in another village. Fei's aunt glowered at me with such menace that all I wanted was to be swallowed up by the bed frame and disappear. "I know your kind. Layabout good-for-nothing. A dreamer, like your father." She started toward me, her fist raised.

"Leave him alone!" Fei wailed, but she was silenced by a sharp tug on her ear. Shu cuffed the girl across the mouth with the other hand.

"I will have none of your disobedience—you understand?"

There was a long silence, and then Fei nodded, mute except for sniffles and sobs. I managed to stagger to my feet, but I stopped short when I caught Fei's eye. A sharp warning, as if to say, *You'll only make it worse.*

Finally, Shu let her go. Fei sobbed and clutched at her ear as her aunt stalked out. She hesitated by the door, and her head tilted so that I just caught a glimpse of her profile, eyelashes weighed down by her tears.

But she didn't turn to look at me as she followed her aunt out the door.

★ ★ ★

I thought about going after her, or at least trying to find her house so I could see if she was okay. But the longer I debated it, the more impossible it seemed. I could picture that final look she'd given me, which had screamed *stay away.*

Days later, the water jug grew slimy again, and there was nothing but ash in the stove. The rest of the sweet potato was gone. My stomach ceased to growl, like it knew there was no use in complaining, and the watery mush we'd shared was nothing but a faded memory. But the girl—the girl stayed in my thoughts, tangled with my dreams.

One day, there was another knock at the door.

I rushed to open it, but no one was there. I looked up and down the path and sniffed, certain I could catch a whiff of her unique earthy scent.

But there was only a small, deformed sweet potato left on the step.

PART I

上山下乡

Up to the Mountains
and Down to the Villages

SUMMER, 1968

CHAPTER 1

MING

The morning was already sticky and wet. Steam rose from the puddles that had collected along the roads during the last rains. I was running, my back sweaty, my hair hanging in my face. I huffed at it, and the strands flew upward, then settled in my eyeline again.

"Ming, Ming, wait up!" a voice called from behind me. I wasn't the only one late this morning.

Tian caught up, his unbuttoned work shirt flapping around him, an unlit cigarette dangling from his mouth.

"Little brother, what's the rush? We all receive the same bag of manure no matter what time we arrive." He pinched the cigarette from his lips and tucked it behind his ear.

"Easy for you to say," I replied with a smile. "We all know you're the Cadre's favorite." Tian laughed and shoved me playfully.

"Come on, slowpoke," he chided as he took off for the work hall.

As we ran through the village, the shirts clinging to our backs were drenched in moments. Typhoon season was just around the corner, which would bring welcome relief after the hot summer months in Dingzai village and the rest of Dapeng.

The work hall was in the center of the village. It was where we checked in with our team leader every morning and was also where we reported at the end of the day and received our daily work points. We all worked in the fields from early in the morning until it was too dark to see. Digging, planting, picking—every day was the same, with rare breaks on the few public holidays.

As we neared the hall, I saw that we weren't quite the last ones to check in for the morning.

"There's trouble," Tian murmured, taking the cigarette from behind his ear and tucking it safely into the carton he kept in his shirt pocket. A group of boys lingered by the entrance to the hall. Caocao, the tallest, turned and spotted us.

"You stink-breaths are late." Caocao ambled over to me. The tips of my ears were on fire, and I dropped my head as the gang around him sniggered. "That's a deduction of at least one work point each." My heart stopped; one full work point was about a week's worth of field work.

Caocao wouldn't have picked on us this way if our fathers were around. He seemed to have it in for the orphans while his own dad was the most powerful man in the village—Caocao was the Cadre's son, and he made sure we never forgot it.

"Mind your own business, Caocao," Tian said. "No one made you brigade leader."

Caocao smacked his lips, his eyes narrowing like a hawk homing in on its prey. "Brigade Leader's a busy man. He needs some help to keep bastards like you in line. He'll know about your tardiness before long." He squeezed his fist until his knuckles cracked.

"What do you want?" I asked, wishing he'd just leave us alone.

"It's been a lean month; the boys and I could use a little extra." The boys around us grinned eagerly. "One grain coupon each ought to cover it."

My hands automatically went to my pockets. It was only when I held a coupon in my fist, worth a precious half kilo of grain, that I realized Tian hadn't moved a muscle.

"Tian," I whispered, elbowing him in the side. "Come on." But Tian shook his head and squared his jaw, pulling himself up so he was looking the other boy in the eye.

Caocao leaned forward so his broad, flat nose almost bumped Tian's. "You know, I don't like your attitude, but I'm willing to overlook it. How about a couple of those American-import cigarettes?"

And then Tian smiled. "Sik si laa," he spat.

I felt the blood drain from my face as Caocao went purple. Tian didn't even blink, the corners of his mouth curling up ever so slightly. I felt the press of bodies as the boys surged forward, ready to teach us a lesson.

"Good morning, comrades." The loudspeakers crackled to life above our heads.

We all froze. Instead of the usual propaganda slogans, the Cadre himself was addressing the village.

"My fellow comrades, this is a message from your esteemed Party. Field work is delayed this morning for an important announcement. Report to the assembly area in ten minutes, no exceptions. That is all."

Tian and I exchanged a look of alarm, and even Caocao's boys were distracted. An official announcement was hardly ever good news.

Caocao jerked his head, and the group dispersed, but my sigh of relief was cut short. "This is not done."

Tian smirked, and I had half a mind to scold him for giving Caocao a new reason to hassle us. Before I could say anything, he clapped me on the shoulder and took off. "Come on, we don't want to be late twice in one morning."

I went after him, and we joined the rest of the villagers for the ominous assembly.

CHAPTER 2
MING

The villagers jabbered and gossiped even as the Cadre took the stage with three other senior Party officials from Long-chi. The stage was simply an area of marked concrete under a basketball hoop missing its net. The entire village of two hundred or so men, women, and children, minus the bedridden, were crammed onto the court and the tiny amphitheater beside it, spilling out onto the grass nearby. Another speaker towered over our heads, like the one outside the work hall, more were placed all around the village and even within earshot of the fields. Even though nobody had running water or electricity, there was a lone generator that was used for official Party business, and that included powering the speaker system. The village was often blasted with Party announcements and declarations and called to work or formal gatherings like this one.

The Cadre cleared his throat and held up a hand for silence, but the villagers mostly ignored him. These speeches usually went on for too long and were too vague to hold everyone's attention.

I noticed the unfamiliar men standing behind the Cadre and Party officials in their faded navy work uniforms. Two of them, both stern and glowering, were dressed in thick green army jackets. The third wore a long winter coat lined with fur. His hair was slicked back. He stared out over the crowd, his waxed mustache twitching. He held himself erect and proud, so he seemed much taller than the men beside him.

Tian shifted restlessly, smoking a cigarette, but I was getting more and more curious. We hardly ever got any news about what was happening in the rest of the country, and I'd only ever managed to get my hands on a few pages from newspapers, which I kept hidden away under my mattress. I cherished those articles and scraps of news because they offered glimpses into life beyond the village, something I could only imagine.

"Comrades!" The Cadre's voice was high-pitched and sharp. Tian liked to snigger that he should be in the opera, playing a young girl, with his lovely eunuch's falsetto.

"We have the honor to do a great service to our state and to further the great revolution of our Party." He puffed his chest and slammed his fist into his hand, probably to impress the officials, but the sweat beading on his head and his nasal voice didn't help. Tian chortled, and I bowed my head, trying to control my giggles, but I couldn't keep my shoulders from shaking. The Cadre droned on, saying something about the glorious future of the Party, but neither of us could hear much over our own laughter.

The Cadre moved aside, and the mustached official stepped forward. He was taller than the Cadre and softer, his face smooth and fleshy, not weather-beaten like those of our village Party members. He raised a hand, and I noticed his fingers were long, slim, and smooth. Those hands worked at a desk, not out in the fields.

"Comrades!" His voice boomed, his accent crisp and clean, in marked contrast to the sound of our local dialect. We fell silent straightaway. "Village comrades, soon you will have the chance—the opportunity—to answer your true calling. You will complete an important mission in the service of our glorious country and its people." He swept his arm through the air, his penetrating gaze scanning the crowd.

"In the words of our great Chairman, '*The people, and the people alone, are the motive force in the making of world history.*'"

I knew the quote. Earlier in the year, we'd all been issued copies of *Quotations from Chairman Mao Zedong*. As far as I knew, the book was gathering dust in most of the villagers' homes. Maybe a few had been put to use, wedged under the leg of an uneven stool. More than a few villagers had probably looked at the crisp pages and considered using them as kindling. Probably even more texts would have met that very fate if we hadn't all been warned that the Cadre and Party could conduct random home inspections to search for illicit or counterrevolutionary materials. So we kept the books, if only for the sake of appearances.

I had thought the book would contain important answers— the secrets to what made someone a good citizen, a good Communist, a good Chinaman. But despite poring over the passages I could decipher, I hadn't unlocked any answers.

The official waited for a long beat, as if to emphasize his power and command, before lowering his arm to continue. "Our benevolent and beloved leader, the great Chairman Mao Zedong, has bestowed the most honorable task upon the men and women of the Guangdong province. You will be responsible for the enlightenment and reeducation of our educated youth. They have fought valiantly for the victory of our party, our people, and our revolution, and now they will take their final steps. My brothers and sisters, the great people of this village have been given the honor of carrying out this program.

"Your city comrades will be arriving in the coming weeks, and I expect the most humble and courteous welcome for your brothers. It will be your privilege to pass on the wisdom you have gathered in these fields, and the humility and great strength of character that is common to the people of China. Up to the mountains, down to the villages. They will be coming to the countryside to learn from you, comrades. You will be our pride and joy, the final teachers of the revolution embodying the very soul of the Communist Party!"

He raised his arm again. We were silent. Tian was worrying

at his lip, his expression twisted as he tried to work out the meaning of the tangle of phrases. The other villagers looked just as perplexed.

The Cadre raised his hands above his head and began to clap and nod vigorously. His fellow officers followed suit, softly at first, but quickly gaining in volume after a sideways glance from the Cadre. Everyone put their hands together enthusiastically. Some people let out cheers and whistles.

Tian kept his hands by his sides, refusing to join the applause. "What's he on about?"

But before I could answer, the Cadre raised his fist and started to chant, "Shangshan xiaxiang." *Up to the mountains, down to the villages.* The villagers repeated it with fervor, pumping their fists. Tian didn't chant, but I shouted alongside my neighbors so as not to stick out or appear contrary.

The official nodded his approval, and the Cadre saluted, relief obvious in his stance and gestures. He took the stage once again.

"As we have lost an hour in the fields, your day's work points will be adjusted accordingly." I was ahead for the month, so I didn't care, but I heard groans of dismay from the crowd, which the Cadre ignored. "Please report to your teams."

And just like that, it was over. The visiting officials disappeared, flanked by the Cadre and the local Party members.

"Jau mou gaau co. What was that all about?" Tian cussed loudly. "What's this *up mountain, down village* crap? More new slogans. I need my points!"

As we walked back to the work hall, I tried to explain to him that the village would be hosting a team of city youths—former Red Guards, by the sound of it. I'd heard a bit about the brazen Party youths who had taken control of the cities in the name of the Chairman's Cultural Revolution. They were mostly university and high school students who had managed to overthrow the adult administrations of their institutions. As a result, the city schools were shut down, and now practically all the students had taken up the cause. They called themselves the Red Guards, and Mao Zedong had given them his endorsement, like an unofficial version of the People's Liberation Army. From what I could tell, most of their "work" for the Party involved chanting slogans, putting up posters, and stirring up fervor against anyone deemed counterrevolutionary.

Last year, a couple of Red Guards had stopped by the village as part of a recruitment drive. They wore bright red armbands with bright yellow letters proclaiming their Red Guard status over green uniforms tipped with red on the collars. The pair had spotted Tian and me walking through town. "Come join the glorious Army and further Chairman Mao's great Cultural Revolution." They had shoved a pile of pamphlets under our noses. They all featured the same few drawings of smiling youths, proudly showing off their red armbands as they raised their red books high in the air.

As we studied the flyers, trying to make out the words, the boys before us burst into song.

We are the Red Guards of Chairman Mao,
our red heart steeled in storms and waves.
Armed with Mao Zedong Thought,
we dare to storm mountains of swords and seas of flames.

They clapped their hands above their heads like school-children being led in morning songs. Tian and I exchanged looks and pocketed the pamphlets to use as kindling later.

Despite that first encounter with the Red Guards, I thought the announcement was pretty exciting. It would be fun to have more people our age in the village—from the big city, no less—although I shared Tian's view on needing work points.

Before long, we'd signed in, picked up our tools, and were out in the fields. The sun was high above, beating down on our sweaty backs, and we settled in to work through the steaming day. It was midsummer, which meant harvesting and drying the millet crops. The women crisscrossed the fields with baskets, plucking the ripe pods from their stems, while the men cut down the plants and bundled them up for hay.

By evening, we had all but forgotten about the odd group of city officials and their announcement. There was no more talk of Red Guards or chanting of Party slogans, just the end of another grueling day.

★ ★ ★

At night, the rest of the villagers retired to their homes for a modest dinner. Tian and I shared a dormitory with two other boys, Wang and Cho. I had moved in with them after a couple of months living by myself. Having lost almost a third of the villagers to famine during the Three Years of Natural Disasters, the Cadre and the Party decided it would be easier if the orphan boys all shared a residence, so they had moved us into some of the empty houses in the main part of the village.

Wang was an orphan, like Tian and me, while Cho's parents had left to work in the city, leaving him behind with his grand-mother. When she died, they never came back for him, so he moved in with us.

The four of us were our own little family, although Tian was the closest thing I had to a brother. He shared a small room with me while Wang and Cho slept in the other, and we all used the tiny front alcove as a common kitchen. Tian looked after me, trying to make sure I was involved in games and conversations with the other boys, because I was still so shy. If it weren't for Tian, I'd have been truly alone.

That evening, I left the others playing cards and wandered down to the beach. I walked past our old mud house but didn't bother to go inside. It had taken me a while to get used to living with the others, so in the early years, I had come back often. But now I very rarely turned up the gravel pathway: only when I was feeling particularly lonely.

Instead, I kept walking until I could hear the sea kissing the rocks along the headland. The waves seemed to whisper as they lapped the sand. I sat on the rocks to eavesdrop on their secrets.

Ours was an old fishing village set on a peninsula. Some families still earned their living from the sea, but the majority were farmers like my parents. While most of the villagers knew how to swim, my father had had a particular affinity for the water; he always said that there was nothing wiser than the sea.

When I was four, he'd taught me to swim in a little pool at the edge of the beach, protected from the rough waves. I became a strong swimmer, even trying my luck diving for pearls on the rocky floor of the bay. The other boys my age, including Tian, were always daring one another to try holding our breaths until our lungs burned and the pressure in our noses burst the delicate vessels in our nostrils so that they bled in the water as we tried to dislodge the sharp shells. We never found any pearls, of course.

Tonight, with the end of summer nearing, the water was cool and refreshing, washing away the day's layers of dirt and sweat.

I floated on my back, gazing at the stars and thinking about my father.

During one of our swimming lessons, I was testing how long I could hold my breath underwater. I loved skimming below the surface, feeling the bubbles of my breath pop against my face.

"All you need is a set of gills, and you could swim to Hong Kong," Ba had said.

"Why would I swim there?" I had visions of diving for pearls and finding treasure chests left behind by warlords and pirates.

Swimming to an island didn't seem that interesting, and I said as much.

My father had smiled. "Treasures and trinkets may be valuable, but there is no price you can put on what Hong Kong can offer a village man like you or me."

"What's that?"

"Freedom."

★ ★ ★

A slap across my right cheek startled me from my reverie. I lifted my head in time to see a silver tail disappearing into the murk. The fish was quick, but I was faster. I cupped my hands and lifted it out of the water, creating a cage with my fingers so it couldn't flop out.

When I felt the slippery body still, I snuck a peek. It was a small thing, maybe a mackerel or even a large minnow, caught between my palms, its gills billowing uselessly.

I closed my hands again and carefully maneuvered to the side of the pool, then leaned over to plunge my arms into the sea. The body stirred, sharp fins digging into my skin. I brought my head down so my lips were almost touching the water.

"Swim, my friend. Swim to freedom."

I pulled my fingers apart, breaking the cage. There was a silver flash, and it was gone, washed away by a wave. I smiled as I pictured the thin body swimming against the current, dodging the sharks that plagued these waters, pushing out toward the open sea.

三

CHAPTER 3
MING

We were out in the fields when we heard the trucks coming in. Three of them, pulling up slowly and rocking from side to side. There hadn't been a vehicle in Dingzai for months, and we all dropped our tools to watch as they approached the work hall. The driver of each truck hopped down and pulled aside the canvas covering the back, and, one by one, shy figures emerged.

Our city youths had arrived.

"Any girls?" Tian was at my side, shielding his eyes from the sun. It was hard to tell from this distance, with all their bodies hidden under stiff new village work uniforms. Gone were their green military uniforms and caps, though a few of them still had red bands around their arms, the only physical evidence left of their former Red Guard status.

One of the red bands came to the front—probably a boy, by the way he walked—and raised a hand. All at once, the rest of the group spread out in a neat row. The boy seemed to be barking instructions, but we could barely make out his lips moving and had no idea what he might be saying.

"Hey! Get back to work!" The team leader had caught us shirking, which meant point deductions for sure. I scooped up my knife, but Tian had other ideas.

"I'm going to go see."

"But what about—" He cut me off with a wave, reaching for his front pocket as he strode over to the team leader.

"Smoke break, sir." The leader eyed him warily but accepted one of the cigarettes Tian waved at him. Tian helped him light up before lighting his own. The supervisor dismissed him with a grunt.

Tian winked at me before scampering away.

As tempted as I was to join him, I had nothing to offer the leader. So I hunched back over, hacking away at the millet plants with long, swift strokes, like in the old kung fu movies they used to screen for the villagers in the work hall before the Cultural Revolution, before they were replaced by the Party-endorsed operas.

When the horn blared for lunch, I dropped my tools and headed back to the dormitory.

I pushed open the door, calling out, "Hey, Tian, did you find—"

Four lean, curious faces peered back at me.

"Who are you?" the tallest boy demanded.

"Who are *you*?" I said without thinking. "What are you doing in my room?"

"Cadre put us here. Are you from the village?" His accent was smooth and crisp, a city voice. Maybe Guangzhou.

I nodded, and the four strangers exchanged looks. I wanted to shrink into myself. Where was Tian when I needed him?

"I'm Li," the boy said. He was a good head taller than I was. To my surprise, Li flashed a warm, friendly smile and offered me his hand. I realized I had never shaken anyone's hand before. Villagers hardly ever greeted each other with such formality— just a short bow or a nod of greeting, and kowtowing for more formal occasions like weddings.

I hesitated before reaching out. The boy's grip was firm, but his fingers were soft and unblemished. I felt ashamed of the grime that coated my skin.

"I'm Ming," I said awkwardly, unsure whether to return the pressure of Li's grip or let go. I waited until Li pumped our joined hands twice and then dropped my arm back to my side. Li gestured to the group. "This is Feng, Kamshui, and Ah-Jun." The boys nodded in turn. They all looked the same to me—tall and thin with smooth skin. They had the same expression of curiosity and pity.

I did my best to smile wide like Li, but it felt like I was just trying to show off the crowdedness of my teeth.

"So, this is it?" Ah-Jun said, taking in the modest room. He spoke the same regional dialect, but his voice was higher pitched. "There's not even glass in the windows."

I blushed and shuffled my feet, not sure if he was expecting me to answer. Evidently not, as Feng chimed in.

"It's simple, humble. Timber and earth and the hard work of the people." He was shorter than his friends, but he held himself tall. He belted out his words, as if each one was of great importance. "If it's good enough for our peasant brethren, it's good enough for me." He strode up to the wall and slapped it with an open palm. The little building shook, showering us with bits of dust and gravel.

"Easy there, comrade." Li chuckled softly. "You don't want to take down the entire village on our first day. There's more than enough work to do."

My ears perked up. "Work?" I asked, suddenly conscious of my own yowling compared to the boys' smooth, purring speech.

Li smiled. "That's right. We will be offering our assistance to your village, working side by side with our brothers to ensure a productive labor force. We will, of course, be looking to you to show us how best to complete the tasks at hand."

I nodded, still getting used to the unique lilt of his voice. "How many of you are there?"

"Thirty in this early group, spread over Dapeng," Feng replied. "We're lucky to be among the first." The others' expressions made me wonder if they really saw themselves as lucky.

"That's right," Li said. "Most of us are from Guangzhou, though some heeded the call from other parts of the province." He flashed that winning smile again. "*Up to the mountains, down to the villages.* Your area is one of the first to take part in the Party's new program."

"Um, it's an honor," I said, though I wasn't sure what it all meant. I glanced around the suddenly cramped room, noticing that an extra set of bunk beds had already been moved in, with backpacks and clothes strewn on them. My eyes fell on a familiar-looking red cover.

"*Quotations from Chairman Mao Zedong*—we have that too." I pointed to the book.

Li stooped to retrieve it. "The only words you need to know. The only words *worth* knowing these days," he said with a bright smile, handing the book to me. I traced the letters on the cover. Unlike mine, which still looked brand-new, this book was well thumbed.

"So, uh, you guys must read a lot?" I said, brushing my fingers over the worn silhouette of Mao.

Feng narrowed his eyebrows. "What are you implying? Don't you know Chairman Mao Zedong himself says, '*To read too many books is harmful*'?"

My face felt like it was on fire. "I . . . I just mean you must read newspapers and all that. You know, like the *People's Daily* or the *Worker's Daily* . . ."

"Oh, don't tell me you buy into the rubbish in the *Worker's*

Daily!" Ah-Jun shook his head. "There are only three papers worth the pages they are printed on: the *People's Daily, Liberation Army Daily*, and *Red Flag*." My ears burned with shame at my ignorance.

"No need to confuse the boy," Feng said before turning to me. "You don't need to worry. Just study Mao Zedong's wise teachings; they will deliver us from our bourgeois past toward the great rebirth."

Li went over and clapped his friend on the shoulder. "Sorry, Ming," he said. "Comrade Feng here likes to spill vernacular, mistaking himself for a politician." The other boys laughed, even Feng. I gave a small smile.

Li flashed me another lopsided grin. He was good-looking. I wondered if he had a girlfriend in the city. No one in the village would even think of having a relationship until they were ready to marry—around eighteen—but I knew things were different in the city. There, maybe, *maybe* I could talk to Fei.

"So, Ming, which of Chairman Mao's doctrines do you find most meaningful?" Li asked.

My mouth went dry, and I swallowed hard, gaping like a stranded fish. "I . . . I . . . I . . ."

Just then, the door burst open. "Boys!" a voice boomed. "The long-awaited army has finally arrived."

I heaved a sigh of relief as Tian bounded into the room.

Tian was already addressing everyone, his hands clasped in front of him in the old-fashioned imperialist greeting, not like my awkward handshake with Li. He grinned broadly like a seasoned host. "Welcome, welcome to our humble village." He paused when he came to Li.

"What, they've got the movie stars down here now too?" Tian quipped. Li flashed him a good-natured smile. "So much for the girls; we don't stand a chance around this one." Tian clapped the taller boy on the shoulder, like an old friend.

"Comrade, you can rest assured that my only interest here is to further the cause," Li said with a laugh. "I'm Li."

"I'm Tian. Welcome . . . comrade," he added. I had never heard him sound so formal before. He must have been eager to impress. "So, what's the story, boys? Are there any girls coming?"

The group chuckled.

A knock came at the door, and without waiting for a response, a city boy with a red armband poked his head around the frame. "Time for a Party meeting," he barked. He drew back when he saw Tian and me.

"Who's this?" He addressed the new boys, not us.

"They're local boys," Li offered. "Ming and Tian, this is Commander Hongbing, our squad leader."

Hongbing huffed and paid us no further attention. "We have a meeting in the hall in fifteen minutes." He cast Tian and me another sidelong glance. "And I'm sure your *comrades* have their own duties to attend to."

I swallowed and was about apologize and agree, but Tian elbowed me in the side before I could.

"Aye, Commander Hongbing." The other boys rose and followed their leader out, but Li paused by the door. He lifted his clasped hands in the same imperial style Tian had.

"See you soon," he said. Tian laughed and returned the farewell.

"I like him," Tian declared, throwing himself down on the bed Feng had just been sitting on. He reached for a backpack.

"Hey, that's not ours," I said, but it was too late. Tian was already rummaging through the pockets.

"Clothes, papers, boring." He tossed the offending items aside. "Where is the good stuff? Don't these city boys have comic books and magazines?" He picked up the red book. "Who's this guy? Check out his jowls—like those men in them salty-wet cartoons where the girls all have dai tofu." He mimed lewdly, and I rolled my eyes.

"That's *Quotations from Chairman Mao Zedong*—the Little Red Book," I said, reaching for the book, but he batted my hand away. "They gave us all that book. Don't you remember?"

"*A revolution is not a dinner party, or writing an essay, or painting a picture, or doing embroidery,*" Tian read in his halting voice, mispronouncing half the words. "What is this crap? Painting a picture? I can paint you a picture." I snatched the book from him as he reached for the particular part of his anatomy he was going to "draw" with.

"Stop it, what's wrong with you?" I smoothed the pages and

returned the book to the bag. "You can't say stuff like that around these guys. It's . . . you can't. You just can't."

"What was all that bourgeois crap they were talking about?" Tian scoffed, also mispronouncing *bourgeois*. He must have been listening outside the door, I realized. "They're a bunch of spoiled brats who think they can fight wars and feed themselves with words." He spat on the ground, and a wet star glistened on the dirt floor. "I'll show them what they can do with their Little Red Book." He reached for the book again, intending to align it with the backside of his trousers before I yanked it from his grasp.

"You are such a troublemaker," I exclaimed, and he laughed.

"All right, come on. We better head back to the fields before this lot starts taking over."

★ ★ ★

We didn't see the boys for the rest of the afternoon. The trucks that had brought them rattled back down the road.

At dinnertime, Tian and I returned to the dormitory early. It was our turn to prepare the evening meal. There wasn't much to go around, and our cooking skills paled in comparison to our memories of our mothers, but we made the most of it.

But when I opened the door, a fine feast was already laid out. There were bowls of rice and at least three vegetable dishes. It was as much food as we would have had to celebrate the New Year.

Li stood over the little stove, ladling out hot broth.

"Tian, Ming, welcome home. I hope you're hungry," he said with a smile. There was no table, so Feng, Ah-Jun, and Kamshui had laid everything out on the floor of the tiny alcove we used for a kitchen. "Please take a seat," he added, pointing.

I wasn't sure what to think. No one had cooked for us since our parents, and we were all precious about rations and coupons. Why were these new arrivals being so generous? I swallowed and looked helplessly at Tian. His face said nothing, but his eyes were hard. Then he just shrugged and moved to squat. Wang and Cho were already seated, their grins stretching as they eyed the spread.

Li waited until we had settled in before placing bowls of broth before us. "We thought we would prepare dinner for you boys as a way of thanking you for the warm welcome to your home!" He grinned wide, his teeth shining bright white.

"Wow, fat pork meat!" Wang reached to pinch a piece of pork, but Cho slapped his friend's hand away.

"This is the last of our city rations. Commander Hongbing explained that we'll have to stick to the village diet from now on, so we thought we would have one last feast. Please, help yourselves," Li said before plunging his chopsticks into his rice bowl.

I picked up my own chopsticks. Wang, Cho, and Tian dove straight in, but I was suddenly feeling shy.

Meanwhile, Li ate heartily, his chopsticks making soft *tings* against the sides of the bowl. The other boys were eating away, and I awkwardly scraped some rice and meat into my bowl.

The food was delicious; it had been months since I'd had any meat. I wondered whether the city boys ate like this every day and felt a pang of jealousy as I remembered Fei's tiny sweet potatoes.

Li finally set his nearly empty bowl back on the table. "So, where are the rest of the villagers?" he asked good-naturedly.

"They eat at home," Tian said with his mouth full.

"I thought the villagers would all eat together. Communal dining in the true spirit of Communism. It was one of Chairman Mao's core ideas," Ah-Jun said with a frown.

"That was stopped ages ago," I muttered into my bowl.

"Surely a village like this is the perfect place for the true order of Communism, the commune, to thrive?" Feng said. He glared at me, as though expecting me to explain the village's counter-revolutionary betrayal.

I kept my attention on my bowl of food. These boys didn't understand. How could they? The Three Years of Natural Disasters had decimated our village. By the end of the first year, the communal cook was boiling stones in the giant stockpots.

Tian cleared his throat. "The villagers just stopped coming," he said, trying his best to sound matter-of-fact. "There was no food."

Li set down his bowl and straightened. He was so tall that even sitting down, it felt like he was standing at a podium. "Well, I, for one, am honored to be sharing this meal with my dearest brothers and our newest comrades. To share our food and to share our home. And I hope that the other villagers may see fit to join us in time in the true spirit, not just of Communism, but friendship."

His smile was so bright and welcoming, I couldn't help giving him a small nod.

Tian raised his cup of watered-down tea. "To friendship," he said, and the eight of us clinked our mugs together.

四

CHAPTER 4

MING

After our bountiful dinner, I went down to the shore. I dunked my head under the water to clear it but couldn't shake my thoughts of the new arrivals.

Li especially stood out to me. He didn't speak like the other boys. He was thoughtful and considered, and his eyes had light in their depths, like sparkling fish.

When I returned to the dorm, Wang and Cho had retired to their room along with Ah-Jun and Kamshui. But I was surprised to find Tian poring over the Little Red Book he had found on Feng's bed. Feng was sprawled out beside him, Li on his other side.

"*Politics is war without bloodshed, and war is politics with bloodshed,*" Feng recited, eyes closed. "*Also, political work is the lifeblood of all economic work.*" Tian was frowning, tongue poking out the corner of his mouth as his finger trailed along the page. Li reached over and gently tugged Tian's hand down two lines so that he was in the right spot.

"What he means is that we are always engaged in a war of ideas and must stay wary so we won't be misled by false ideals," Feng continued, his eyes snapping open as I perched on the side of the bed next to Li. "The only way to stay the true course is to study Mao's teachings and to recite his work daily. I've memorized the whole Red Book, but I still recite passages every day so I can be certain I am thinking with a Communist mind and that my thoughts and actions are in the best interests of the Party."

"Wah, I can't imagine knowing a whole book," Tian murmured, staring down at the neat rows of characters that packed the page. "It would take me a whole week just to read a page."

"Nonsense, it's easy." Li showed Tian some of the basic radicals and structures for the characters in the lines.

"*Women . . . hold up . . . level . . . sky*," Tian read, halting and squinting after each character. Li nodded in encouragement. I peeked over Tian's shoulder.

"Half the sky," I couldn't help correcting him. "See, that's *half* because the dots are over the two lines. Level is like this." I used my finger to draw the character that looked to me like a scowling face peering over a fence. That was how I remembered it.

"You're a good scholar," Li said, his face brightening. "Have you ever thought about going to senior school or university?"

I blushed and shook my head. "Nah, after the first four years, I stayed home to help my family in the fields. I learned to read mostly from newspapers, when I could find them. I started collecting interesting articles; I still have some."

Li's face brightened. I fetched the bundle of pages I kept under the bed, Li following behind me.

"These are some of the most important pieces in history," he said as he riffled through my collection. "The political thoughts of some of the most notable figureheads of modern Communism."

I pointed to an image under one of the headlines. "I like this one about the student protesting with the big-character poster at Beijing University." The poster read, ANNIHILATE ALL THE MONSTERS AND DEMONS COMPLETELY, THOROUGHLY, AND ENTIRELY.

"That was the start of the big-character poster movement," Li observed.

"Here's the one Chairman Mao wrote himself." I pointed to another image. "Bombard the Capitalist Headquarters: My First Big-Character Poster."

"All of the university students were putting posters up, denouncing reactionaries, and calling the country to arms. To be a good Red Guard, you had to read and put up these posters as part of the revolution," Li explained.

I was suddenly curious. "How do you know? Did you go to university?"

"No, Feng and I were recruited to the Red Guards out of senior school." He nodded to Feng. "Do you remember the head of foreign studies? What a rightist snob."

Feng grimaced. "He got what was coming to him—marching in the streets in a dunce cap, begging for forgiveness. At least he saw the error of his ways." His eyes narrowed. "Unlike that professor of English. Stubborn American intellectual. He called us anarchists."

My mouth was dry. "What happened to him?"

Feng grinned horribly. "Got what was coming to him too." His low voice sent a chill through me. "He wasted his last stubborn breath condemning the revolution. What a pig." And he made a slitting motion across his throat.

The hair on my arms stood on end. Tian's face was frozen, his thoughts unreadable.

Li cleared his throat. "Come now, Feng. Don't be like that. These are our brothers." He tilted his head to me. "He was run out of the school, along with the rest of the administration. There was no place for their line of thinking there," he said solemnly.

My shoulders sagged, and I felt the rush of blood returning to my cheeks. I sighed audibly, and Li laughed, clapping me on the shoulder.

"I was just messing with you boys," Feng said with a smirk, punching Tian on the arm. "You village boys will believe anything."

But Tian's brow was knitted. "I don't have much education, and I can barely read," he said evenly. "But if there's one thing experience has taught me, it's how to spot someone who will lose their life and someone who has taken one."

Li stiffened beside me, and Feng's smile dropped. He stood up and balled his fists by his sides.

"Just what do you know about it, country boy?" Feng hissed. "The Red Guards are here to ensure adherence to Mao's doctrines. If that means a few bourgeois sympathizers take their deserved punishments, then so be it. Like Chairman Mao himself says, politics is war."

Tian stood and stepped forward, his chin high. "You city boys think you know everything. Do you really know what it's like to be surrounded by death? When your life is so insignificant that when you die, your body is eaten by your own family?"

The two boys were standing nose-to-nose, glaring fiercely.

"Let's settle down, comrades," Li said.

Before anyone could say anything more, there was a loud scraping of boots followed by pounding on the door.

"Lights out, comrades." It was Commander Hongbing on a nightly patrol all the way from Long-chi, where he was stationed. I guessed he was taking responsibility for his squad beyond their work in the fields.

I snuffed the kerosene lamp in the corner, and the room plunged into darkness. I thought the commander would come in to check on us, but there was only silence, then footsteps headed away from the dorm.

No one said a word as we all fumbled in the darkness. I felt a little sheepish about how quickly I had rushed to obey, but also relieved. That conversation was getting nasty.

I climbed into my bed and sank into the covers, exhaustion

taking over. The sagging boards creaked above me as Tian climbed into bed without bidding me good night.

I lay in the darkness, taking in the new "silence." The other boys had settled into their own bunk, Feng on top and Li across from me. It was impossible to ignore the extra breathing in the room, the sighs and soft murmurs only an arm's length away from my bunk.

I heard scratching and shifting overhead, and then something fluttered down and landed on my stomach. I picked up the scrap of paper, carefully folded in quarters. It was written in Tian's looping, halting scrawl in the same style as the big-character posters we had been looking at.

Down with Mao's murderers.

I shuddered and crumpled the paper into the tiniest ball I could manage, then swallowed it for good measure. What was Tian playing at? Just thinking those words could get us into insurmountable trouble, never mind writing them. I heard Tian cackling above me, and I resisted the urge to push my foot through the wooden planks and kick him for his foolishness. But there was another voice inside my head that I couldn't shake.

Just who were these Red Guards, and what had they brought to our village?

★ ★ ★

We rose early the next morning, as usual. A chill had settled over the village with the morning mist. Last night's feast was a distant memory, and we were back to eating our cold steamed buns in silence.

While we trudged out to the fields, the city boys were ushered away by Commander Hongbing to tend to their own plot of land. Tian snuck away on smoke breaks throughout the day to spy on them. The boys had been put to work on a sad-looking patch of land, harvesting sweet potatoes. The Cadre had a few of the elderly farmers show the boys how to use spades to dig for the roots of the crop. It was a bit early for harvesting, but I guessed the Cadre felt these new arrivals weren't ready to thrash millet plants.

Tian made frequent reports while we worked—he must have gone through half a pack of cigarettes that day.

"They are worse than children," Tian laughed. "Throwing dirt everywhere, complaining about their backs hurting after a few minutes. They won't last a week."

Dinner was a quiet affair. Tian and I cooked for the four of us, as usual, but the city boys didn't even have the strength to light the stove. Feng was leaning against the wall, his eyes half shut, barely able to lift his mantou to his mouth. The day of labor had clearly taken its toll.

"Won't last a week," Tian whispered to me while we ate.

As night fell and the stars came out, I headed for the beach. The air was nippy; autumn had officially arrived, but the seawater was warming up. The waves bubbled and gurgled like happy children. I plunged in, forcing my eyes open against the sting of the salt water. It was too dark to see much, but I could still pick out the vibrations of aquatic life—the flick of a tail, the wave of a green tendril. In the sea, I was never alone.

But then I realized I actually *wasn't* alone. I surfaced quickly, peering toward the shore. A gangly figure stood on the rocky beach, trousers rolled up to his knees, a grimy towel slung over his shoulder.

Li.

My whole body tensed, annoyed by the intrusion.

"Good evening, comrade," he called. "Nice night for a swim!"

I said nothing. Li stepped closer, the water coming up to his ankles, while I stayed where I was.

"There's no way to take a bath, but I figured a dip in the ocean would be just as refreshing."

I shrugged. Villagers rarely bathed. What was the point if you were just going to get even dirtier the next day?

Li plunged his hands into the water. "Salt water. I would have thought you'd prefer the fresh water of the river. That's close by, isn't it?"

A shiver snaked up my spine, thinking of Ma and the other villagers who'd been left there. I shook my head to clear the image. "I don't go there. No one really does," I said.

"Yeah, that's what I heard." He wiggled his toes in the sand. "Tian said I might find you here."

"Oh." I stood up, letting the water run off me. I was a bit irritated that Tian would divulge my pastimes to this virtual stranger. The cool night air hit my skin, but I resisted the urge to plunge back into the comforting warmth of the sea.

Li paused, looking unsure. Slowly, he stripped off his trousers and his shirt, folding them painstakingly. He didn't glance in my direction, just squared his jaw and clenched his fists before shuffling into the foam.

I leaned back, settling into a lazy dead man's float, and watched him out of the corner of my eye. Li grimaced when the surf hit his calves, and I could see he was deciding how to plunge his whole body in. A deliciously evil thought crossed my mind, but I shook my head. I didn't know this boy well enough to play a prank like dunking him in, not without Tian to back me up. So I just watched as, inch by inch, Li submerged himself.

My ears pricked up as a dull roar approached behind me. I didn't need to look to sense the wave gathering momentum and speed. Li saw it, his eyes fixed above my head, his mouth open. At the right moment, I sucked in a deep breath and threw myself backward, flipping into the swell as it curled and tumbled over me.

The churn of the water was muffled even as it rumbled past my ears, loud and quiet at once. I stayed submerged for a bit, letting the crashing subside completely. Then I shot up, breaking the surface nose first, shaking my head to clear the water from my eyes.

When I could see again, I burst out laughing.

Li was sitting on his bottom, limbs splayed, naked as the day he was born. Water was streaming down his face as he coughed and spluttered. My giggles just got louder as he tried to stand, his legs immediately giving way so he landed on his hands and knees.

"What—what—" His words were lost in a fit of coughing.

I spied something gray bobbing in the water and quickly snagged it. His underwear. I waved it over my head like a flag, whooping and hollering.

"It's the flag of our comrades. We march under its banner to glory."

Li's face broke into a wide grin.

"Very funny, village boy. Hand them over, will you? I haven't gotten my sea legs yet."

I thrashed toward the shore and lobbed the wet drawers toward him. Li got up and put them on. They'd taken quite a beating and billowed around his small frame like a lady's skirt. I snorted, spraying salt water.

Li smiled. "I guess we city boys have a few things to learn."

★ ★ ★

Li and I sat on the beach as he smoked a cigarette from the pocket of the shirt he had stowed on a rock.

"So you can't swim?" I asked, eyeing the offered cigarette between his thumb and forefinger. It had BIG FRONT DOOR printed on the end, one of the good brands that even Tian couldn't get.

I never smoked, not even when Tian insisted, and I handed it back without putting it to my mouth.

"I've never seen the ocean before," Li confessed, puffing little clouds toward the stars.

"I can teach you," I offered, surprising myself. I was usually shy and uncomfortable, even around the villagers, but Li put me at ease.

"That would be . . . much appreciated, comrade." He frowned. "But I'm not sure I'm quite ready for another lesson from the sea."

I gestured toward the sheltered pool. "That's where my father taught me. There are no waves there."

"Like a swimming pool?" Li must have read the blank look on my face, because he shook his head and sighed. "Never mind. Things sure are different here. It's taking some getting used to."

I nodded. "What's the city like?"

Li shrugged. "Crowded. Busy. Lots of people. None of this." He gestured to the landscape. "Everyone lives all cramped and crowded in dormitories. And the other students are all up in your business, even when you go to the toilet."

"Sounds a bit like the village," I said. Li snorted in response, and I smiled.

"Did you . . . did you have a girlfriend?" I was surprised by my bold question, but I was curious about life outside Dingzai. Especially if it could change my standing with Fei.

Li shook his head. "Nothing like that. I was too busy with studies and Red Guard duties. What about you?"

It was my turn to shake my head, staring down at my feet, embarrassed that I had brought it up. But Li pressed on, like he could read my mind. "But you have someone in mind?"

I shrugged. "I . . . know a girl. But her family doesn't approve of me."

"That's too bad," Li said, gazing out at the sea. "It's a shame, really. Society makes us draw these lines between us when in the end, we are all made of flesh and bone."

"This is true. My father used to say, 'It doesn't matter where they're from—all desperate men are the same.'" I watched Li's smoke curl upward and out before disappearing completely, leaving only its sharp scent. I felt light-headed but alive.

"Well, in that case, I hope we'll always be different, brother." Li clapped my shoulder and flashed one of his infectious smiles.

I hope so too, I thought.

五

CHAPTER 5

MING

Even after a week in the fields, it was still a sight to see the city boys hunched over their tools, moving even slower than the old men who were training them. At first, they whined every night, but by the end of that first week, most of them were collapsing into bed too exhausted even to complain.

Li, Kamshui, and Ah-Jun grumbled constantly, rubbing their backs and massaging their feet. But Feng endured the labor surprisingly well. He was also slow, and his grip on his tools was no stronger than a child's, but there was an iron determination in him. With every strike of his pick, it was like he was reaffirming his purpose. He took to chanting Maoisms while he toiled, grunting out the words between gritted teeth.

Hongbing often visited the dormitory to commend Feng for his efforts, and even the Cadre stopped by once to begrudgingly offer his praise. Feng acknowledged the compliments with a salute and a nod.

"*Once all struggle is grasped, miracles are possible,*" he declared, as if he'd been called on in class. The squad leader walked away pleased, but the Cadre just shook his head and mumbled something under his breath.

In the weeks after the boys arrived, the village was abuzz with the approach of the Mid-Autumn Festival. National holidays offered us rare days off from the field. Most of the villagers went to Long-chi, where market stalls and shops would be decorated with paper lanterns. Banners of fine calligraphy featured poems and slogans encouraging a bountiful autumn harvest. People used to take homemade sweets or their own small harvests and sell them on the streets, but now they were afraid of being punished for being "capitalists."

Tian and I rose early on the day of the festival and rushed through our morning meal, wanting to beat the crowds into town.

There was another reason I was so eager to go. It was the only opportunity I had to see Fei.

Almost a year after her aunt Shu had marched her out of our hut, I had finally seen her again. I had been wandering through town, waiting for Tian to return from "secret business," when I heard a familiar voice.

"Yes, Aunt Shu."

She was with three very young boys. Two toddlers were clawing at her trousers while she held a baby in her arms. Her aunt screeched and scolded before raising her hand to slap Fei on the back of the head. I winced in sympathy. Then Fei looked up, and our eyes met.

After all that time wishing and hoping, the only thing I did when I finally saw her was run.

That was years ago, and I still hadn't spoken to her. Instead, I spent a lot of time spying on her. I knew that the three boys she minded were her cousins and that she was living with Aunt Shu. I remembered Shu standing at my door, hands on her hips, poised to attack, and I couldn't help shuddering every time I saw her, so I kept my distance.

Tian and I pedaled our rusty bike into Long-chi. Tian had found the bike by the side of the road a few months back, and the two of us had tried to repair it with what tools and scrap metal we could find—a tricky task, since most of the scrap metal had been turned over to the steel furnaces. With some cleverly placed bits of string and spokes carved from sturdy sticks, the bike rolled, but it leaned precariously to the left, which made it hard to ride alone. Instead, the two of us took turns pedaling while the other rode on the handlebars, leaning to the right to act as a counterweight.

The ride was bumpy as we rolled past fields. A couple of goats stood in the dry patches of grass, ribs protruding from their sides. The livestock had never seemed to fully recover from the famine, even the new ones that were brought in from nearby. No matter how good the grass or how much they grazed, they stayed skinny.

We hit a fork in the dirt road and veered to the left. The path to the right was overgrown with weeds and grass from lack of use. Tian pumped the pedals a little faster. I could just make out the roar of the river that lay at the end of the right fork.

The festival was even busier than usual. Ours wasn't the only village with new arrivals, and it looked like villagers from all around the district were keen to share their observations of the youths assigned to them. There were more goods for sale than I'd seen in a while; the villagers must have seen the new arrivals as potential customers.

Tian and I wound our way through the narrow streets, past a group of men squatting on the ground playing a noisy gambling game with marked sticks of bamboo. It was early still, but they had probably been gambling since dawn and would likely stay the rest of the day.

The roads in town were smoother, unlike the rocky tracks of our village, so it was easy to roll our rickety bike along. We passed a rickshaw puller hauling a load of mud bricks, probably to someone building a house nearby.

Tian and I found a spot in the center of the market next to a statue of an old government official from imperial times. We had no idea who he was supposed to be, but he resembled the elderly head teacher from our early school days, so we nick-named him Old Lao.

We sank to the ground under Old Lao, keeping the bicycle close by. Tian dug into his pocket and lit his first cigarette of the day. I leaned against the lumpy base of the statue, ignoring the concrete digging into my back, and shut my eyes. It was nice to just sit for a moment.

"Hey, look, look. They're coming," Tian hissed, whacking me on the arm. I gazed out to where he was pointing. The local girls were walking up the path, a tight circle of them, all wearing the same shapeless gray shirts and trousers. They traveled in a pack, as most girls in the villages did, giggling and gossiping and pretending not to notice the stares from the local boys. A couple were pushing cheap, flimsy bikes. With their small hands gripping the handlebars and their braids flouncing behind them, they may as well have been a royal procession.

In the middle of the group, with two girls clinging to her elbows, was Fei. I sucked in a breath as I watched her laugh and toss her head. I could just make out her voice, like dainty bells.

"Fei!" Her name caught in my throat. I tried again. "Fei!"

I watched her turn, half a head taller than the rest of the girls. Her braid arched gracefully, like a dancer's ribbon, as she sought out the voice.

She caught my gaze, and her eyes lit up for just a moment and then immediately darkened. She looked around, checking her surroundings, and then her lips pulled apart as if to speak.

The short girl with blunt pigtails by her side scowled at me and tugged Fei toward her, hissing something in her ear.

Fei glanced down at her friend and then back at me. She swallowed and shook her head.

"Come on." The pigtailed girl shot me a suspicious glare before steering her friend away.

The girls marched past us underneath the statue. When they got to the other side of the square, Fei broke away from the group, giving her friends a small wave before dashing down the narrow alleyway where I knew she lived with her aunt and cousins.

Tian nudged me in the ribs and gave me a challenging look, as if to ask, *Today?*

I took a deep breath and clenched my fists. Tian didn't know it, but I had made up my mind the night before. It would be my seventeenth birthday next week. It had been more than six years since Fei had shown up at my door, and since that evening sitting out on the rocks with Li, I had wondered why I was so scared. My father's actions may have been a black mark against me in the village, but that didn't have to keep me from talking to her. As Li had said, we were all flesh and bone.

So yes, today would be the day.

Tian shook his head in disbelief as I got up and smoothed down my trousers. But just as I was about to follow Fei down the alley, another group strode into the square.

It was the city boys, all wide-eyed and excited like a litter of puppies. The shopkeepers and farmers were silent, gawking at the sight of them. It wasn't just the group from our village; at least thirty boys had been sent to the area, and this was their reunion. They had changed out of their work clothes and back into their green Red Guard uniforms. There was no mistaking the cleanliness of their garments and clear skin; their urban upbringing shone through in every face.

The boys tried to ignore the staring of the locals. On the edge of the group, Feng spotted us by the statue. He seemed surprised to see us, but instead of coming over, he turned to address the group.

"Comrades, brothers, we must be of service to our community today and assist our new neighbors and friends," he shouted, and the boys' chatter died away. "We have worked hard already, this is true, but like the Chairman says, '*Youth is like the sun at eight or nine o'clock in the morning.*' We are young, we are able, and we have purpose—we are here to learn and help our peasant neighbors."

There were a few murmurs from the boys, some complaints, but mostly, they seemed to agree with Feng's speech. Feng began splitting up the boys, pointing to various tasks and chores throughout the town square and directing the boys to assist with repairs and help clean up. The villagers were completely taken aback as they watched the boys clamber up onto roofs to repair broken tiles and fetch brooms to sweep the streets. They'd been expecting customers, not handymen.

A pair of boys came over. One of them had a few thick whiskers on his chin, which surprised me, as the city boys I'd seen went to great lengths to remain clean-shaven. The boys stopped in front of us and gestured to the statue.

"Hideous," one of them said.

"Deplorable," said the whiskered one. "Get a hammer. He'll have to go."

Tian leapt to his feet, stepping into the whiskered boy's path. "What's wrong with Old Lao?" he demanded.

The city boy glowered. "Don't you know anything, heong haa zai? *'Destroy the Four Olds, Cultivate the Four News.'* This imperialist dog represents the poison that has been fed to the Chinese people for generations and kept us like slaves until Chairman Mao's great revolution."

Tian puffed out his chest. "Don't call our town a dog, you entitled little city—"

Li rushed over. "Comrade Chen, Comrade Sun, there is a pair of elderly women who could use some help fetching water." He pointed to where two stout village grandmothers were striding through the square, clearly having no trouble balancing their loads. The boys exchanged a look but grudgingly went over to help, though the whiskered one gave Tian a hideous sneer.

I raised an eyebrow at Li, but he ignored my unspoken question. "I'm going to check some of the houses across the square, see if they need help with anything," he said. I wasn't sure if it was an invitation, but Tian made no move to leave our spot, so I just nodded mutely. Tian shook his head as the boys around us raced off to do more good.

"I can't believe the garbage they've filled their heads with," he muttered. "Destroy the Olds, my arse."

I didn't reply. The boys had surprised me, most of all Feng. Sure, he was confident and eloquent. But what struck me was how much he really seemed to believe in what he was saying and in the teachings of that little book. I'd opened mine up again, trying to unlock the mystery of how those printed words inspired people like Feng to action. But whatever their power was, it didn't reach me.

Tian got up and seized our bike by the handlebars. "I'm off. See you for lunch," he said, and threw a leg over the seat and wobbled off. That meant he was going to meet up with his "contact"—some dodgy merchant from another town known for dealing in contraband and stolen goods. It was how Tian kept up his supply of bribe cigarettes. I sometimes wondered what Tian could offer in exchange but figured I was better off not knowing.

I was happier on my own anyway. After all, I had a mission to accomplish. I was going to talk to Fei.

My knees felt weak, and my gut shifted so that I had to put an arm out to steady myself against the statue. I blinked a few times to clear my vision.

It was now or never.

Throngs of villagers had arrived now. Little children waved lanterns, and a large crowd watched a pair of pipa and erhu players perform a duet in the square. I squeezed past them, heading to the little alley where Fei had disappeared.

I'd been down this alleyway a few times, and the uneven concrete was familiar beneath my feet. In front of Shu's house, almost at the end of the alley, three small boys were sword fighting with sticks. My ears pricked up when I heard soft laughter, unmistakably Fei's. I walked faster, my heart thumping.

But when I got closer, my stomach twisted tighter and my legs almost gave way.

Fei was not alone. Her head was bent toward the ground, playful and embarrassed. And it wasn't her aunt or one of her friends making her smile. She was laughing with a boy whom I suddenly hated with every ounce of my being.

Li.

He was leering down at Fei, whispering something that made her blush violently. I tried to force myself to look away but couldn't. Li reached a hand toward her, brushing against her arm so that she flinched.

My vision blurred, and hot rage rose up from the pit of my stomach. I gasped aloud, and Li's glance darted in my direction. He started to smile, but his expression turned to confusion when he registered the fury on my face.

I glared, willing the earth to open up and swallow me or for a giant wave to sweep through the alley and carry me away. Or even better, to carry Li away.

Instead, I spun on my heel and ran.

I ran all the way back to the village. My lungs screamed for air and my legs begged to rest, but I couldn't stop. I ran past the village and away from the dormitory, heading toward the ocean. Before I reached the sea, I veered off toward the little boarded-up mud house. I kicked at the door until the old wood splintered and gave way. The single room was full of dust, dirt, and rats' nests, but I didn't care. I sank to my knees in the middle of the floor and wailed. Now I finally understood the old imperial romances, where the forsaken hero found himself contemplating suicide as a result of unrequited love.

The rats skittered out of the house, alarmed by my howling.

I got to my feet, seizing the water jug, and raised it over my head, then brought it crashing down to the ground. The jug clattered away, refusing to break. I yelled again and took hold of the old chamber pot. It was heavy, made of sturdy clay. The pot landed with a booming crack and shattered into ten thousand pieces. Only then did I feel like I had unleashed the whole hurt of my heart.

I collapsed, panting, bits of sharp clay cutting into my skin. Eventually, I stopped feeling pain and just stayed there, staring at nothing.

Footsteps on the gravel cut in on my silence. I had no idea how long I'd been there. For a moment, I thought it was my father returning home from the fields. But the cold floor and shards of shattered clay brought me back to reality. The door creaked open behind me.

"Ming."

I turned toward the familiar voice. My rage had subsided and was replaced by mortification. I didn't want anyone to see me like this, even my oldest friend.

But Tian's eyes were kind. He held the door open, his head cocked. "I haven't seen the inside of this place for a long time." He took in the musty room, the broken shards of clay, and shook his head. "Come on, let's get out of here."

I nodded glumly, wiping my face with the back of my arm. My knees were a bloody wreck, but I felt I'd gotten what I deserved. I couldn't make my feet move toward the door. Tian sighed and stepped inside, meeting me halfway. I wasn't sure how he had known to find me here, but Tian was full of surprises.

"Li said he saw you at the festival."

I stiffened at the mention of Li. The last thing I wanted was the city boys making fun of me.

"What happened?" Tian asked.

But I ignored the question. "Do you think about them?" I whispered. "The way things used to be?" Tian never talked about his family; none of us ever did. The past only danced around in dark shadows and whispers.

"All the time," he said. His tough mask slipped away. "I see Ma and Ba in my sleep, and I see them when I wake up. Sometimes, I think all this, all the stuff that happened—the famine and the Three Years of Natural Disasters—is just a dream. And when I finally wake up, we'll be back at home, and Ma will be doing the washing, and DiDi will be picking his nose and eating it." He had a faraway smile. "But then I go to the fields, and I know this . . . this is it. And we don't talk about it, and we all act like nothing happened. But someone needs to pay. I don't understand the crap they feed us at meetings, but I know that all of this was someone's *fault*." He sighed. "I was hoping maybe the city boys would know more about who was in charge, who had let this happen. But they're too caught up in their posters and slogans about the Olds and News to notice something right under their noses."

I frowned. I had never realized Tian felt this way. He was always joking and playing tough, so his serious side was new to me, and I didn't know what to say.

Tian sighed again. "But what does it matter if we ever find out the truth? In the end, we're going to live and die in those fields."

"What if we didn't? What if we left?" I blurted. Tian's face clouded over. I bit my lip, but the possibility was too tempting to ignore. "What if we went to Hong Kong? If we follow the river upstream—"

Tian seized me by the collar, choking me as he practically lifted me off the floor.

"Are you *kidding* me?" he hissed, shaking me. "How stupid are you?" His eyes darted around the room, searching for spies among the dust and cobwebs. "Don't you ever, ever say something like that again. I don't know what crazy ideas your ba put in your head, but you'll get yourself killed talking like that. If you ever hint at something like that again, I will rip off those puny arms of yours so you never swim another stroke, you understand me?"

I recoiled at the violence in his words, but I knew something else was behind them, stronger than the anger: fear.

We stared at each other for a long while, both of us shaking as he held me by the shirt collar. Finally, I conceded. "Okay. I won't say it again, I promise."

Tian let me go. I rubbed the back of my neck, feeling the blood return. "Let's get back," Tian said finally, pretending nothing had happened. "We can't leave the cooking to Wang. You know how he overcooks the noodles." He tried to smile.

I just nodded, choking back the lump in my throat.

I lingered by the door after Tian left, taking in the small, grimy room, the dust-covered furniture, and the pieces of the shattered chamber pot. I turned away, gently pulling the broken door shut behind me.

六

CHAPTER 6

MING

We'd missed dinner. Wang and Cho had taken pity on the city boys and whipped up some quick noodles and broth for everyone. I wasn't hungry, so I went to bed. My whole body felt heavy, and it was a struggle just to hold my head up.

One minute, I was sinking into my bunk, and the next moment, the loudspeakers were sounding the call to work. I scrambled out of bed and into my clothes, feeling the chill in the morning air.

"Early night, huh?" Li flashed his lopsided grin from the next bunk. My stomach turned, and I had to look away, fighting back the urge to either be sick or cry.

"Morning, laan fan zyu," Tian chimed in. *Sleeping pig.*

Feng and the others had already left, so after a quick breakfast of cold buns, we trudged to the work hall to receive our daily assignments and report to our brigade leader. My head felt foggy, and I was barely thinking when a hand grabbed my shoulder.

"Hey." Li gave me another smile, but I could read the worry in his eyes. "You didn't go to the beach last night."

I glowered at him and tried to yank my arm away, but Li's grip was firm.

"What's the matter?" He pulled his eyebrows together so his smooth movie-star forehead crinkled just so. I noticed his perfect skin, high cheekbones, and long, straight nose. His head had that questioning tilt, and I could see exactly why a girl like Fei would choose him over me. I shook his arm off.

"Li!" Feng found us and slapped his comrade on the back. "Nice work yesterday. The Shu family was particularly taken with you."

"Fei's wonderfully charming and sweet," Li said with a shrug and a grin. "She was telling me how she has never visited the city. I said she was welcome to visit and I'd show her around." I saw a lascivious spark in Feng's eyes.

And before I knew what was happening, my fist was sailing through the air and connecting with Li's perfect face.

Well, it was meant to be his face. At the last moment, he jerked his chin up, so instead of destroying his perfect nose, my knuckles cracked against the front of his throat.

Li reeled back, his eyes wide and desperate as he clutched his neck. I stepped back, horrified, grasping my hand to my chest like I'd burned it.

From nowhere, Tian rushed to Li's side. Li was struggling for breath, and his face was turning purple. "We have to get him to the doctor!" Tian shouted as Li continued to splutter.

Two more boys came over, and the three of them struggled to pick up Li's long, thin body. His jaw was working helplessly, like the minnow I had held in my hands.

I stared as Tian herded the group down the road to the doctor's house.

A few of the villagers setting off to the fields stopped to stare; most of them had missed what had happened, but they still whispered and pointed to me. A wave of nausea passed through me. My face burned with shame, and I took off.

★ ★ ★

It was mid-morning by the time Tian joined me in the fields. My back was soaked, my neck chafed, and my shoulder ached where the cord for the collecting basket dug in. I focused on picking the stalks of grain.

Tian quickly worked his way over to me. He would never make up the time he'd lost, which meant fewer points for the day. I felt even worse.

"He's going to be all right," Tian offered without my asking. "He's having a hard time speaking, but you missed his windpipe. He'll just sound like he swallowed a frog for a while."

The queasiness took hold again, and I said nothing.

"I'm sorry to tell you that he's still as handsome as ever. But thanks for thinking of the rest of us."

My reply was a grunt. Tian was trying to reassure me with his joking, I knew, but the knot in my stomach only tightened.

We worked in silence until the call for lunch came and we

could set down our baskets. Tian made a dash back to the dormitory, but I didn't follow. The guilt had been gnawing at me all morning. I had to see Li.

The doctor, or sifu, as we called him as a sign of respect, worked in town, but he kept basic supplies at his home in the village. We all called his wife Nurse Xi, even though she didn't have any training.

"My dear Ming, how are you?" Nurse Xi greeted me, giving a knowing nod. "You're here to see the Li boy."

I bowed sheepishly, relieved that she didn't press for more details. She had always treated us orphans kindly.

The doctor's house was one of the largest in the village, with two big sleeping rooms, enough space for two large families. Since they didn't have sons or daughters of their own, the doctor's wife used the rooms to care for patients, even letting them stay overnight.

Li was lying on his back on a rickety bed, a washcloth pressed to his neck. He was breathing audibly, the inhales and exhales like an old man's wheezing. He turned when he heard me approaching, and I was surprised when he greeted me with his trademark grin, though there was no masking his wince of pain.

"Hey, it's Flying General Lü Bu," he croaked.

I blushed. Lü Bu was a ruthless general from ancient times who had betrayed his lord. Li's eyes twinkled at the joke, which made me feel even worse.

"I'm sorry, Li. I don't know what came over me," I mumbled. "Are—are you okay?"

Li tried to laugh. "Yeah, nothing some bitter herbs won't fix." He winked, and I realized Nurse Xi was hovering in the doorway; his words were for her benefit. Always the charmer. The thought of him charming Fei twisted my gut.

"I'm glad you're okay." I didn't know what else to say.

I turned to go, but Li reached out and caught my wrist.

"Hey, I've been trying to catch you." He was whispering, and I wasn't sure if it was conspiratorial or out of necessity. I had no choice but to lean over the bed.

"I spoke to that girl yesterday." I felt my hands clench automatically and fought to keep them by my sides. "Fei. She's your friend, isn't she?" My lips wouldn't work, so I just nodded, narrowing my eyes.

"She wanted me to give you something." He let go of my arm and reached into the breast pocket of his shirt, drawing out a carefully folded slip of paper.

My hands were shaking as I unfolded it and saw the tiny neat marks. I'd never seen the handwriting, but I instantly knew who it belonged to.

"It's a letter," Li said matter-of-factly. "She'd been waiting to give it to you but felt shy with her friends around. Your village customs are so strange. In the city, boys and girls just talk to each other." He shook his head. "Anyway, I said I'd be happy to be her messenger, doing my Party duty and all."

I barely heard him as I cradled that slip of paper in my hand like a precious gold leaf. *Fei wrote me a letter. A letter from Fei.*

My heart and spirits soared, and I couldn't stop my smile. Li grinned broadly and then winced in pain. "I feel so stupid, Li," I babbled. "I saw you talking, and I thought . . ."

But Li's eyes were reassuring. "Don't worry about it. You village boys know a thing or two about wooing a girl, don't you?"

I punched him playfully, but Li cried out in surprise and moaned. My hand flew over my mouth in horror. But then he rolled over and let out a wheezy chuckle. Before I could react, he launched himself out of the bed and took a swing. Suddenly, I was in a headlock, held down by Li's surprising iron grip.

Nurse Xi rushed into the room. Li was laughing with no hint of pain at all. I finally managed to break free, and we both sat there, grinning like idiots.

"Well, I'm glad your friend's visit has put you in good spirits," Nurse Xi said. "You're clearly feeling well enough to get back to your duties."

Li sank back into the bed, one arm draped dramatically over his forehead. "Oh, Nurse Xi, I couldn't possibly return to the fields. I must remain here under your gentle care," he gasped.

"Careful, now—those city charms won't work around here." But she came over and used a gentle finger to probe his bruised throat. "Mmm, maybe an afternoon's rest and some more herbs would do you good. Ming, you'll let his squad leader know?" She headed for the door, and Li gave me a wink.

I shook my head and smiled. I clutched Fei's letter and hurried back to the fields.

★ ★ ★

All afternoon, I could feel the letter like a warm stone in my pocket as I hunched over my basket. I was dying to read it, but I couldn't until I was alone.

I set off for the cliffs above the beach as soon as the speakers announced the end of the workday, scrabbling along the headlands until I finally settled onto a rock where I could peer down at the waves crashing below. From here, I could see the seemingly endless expanse of the sea. In the back of my mind, I knew if I could follow its currents all the way around the peninsula, it would take me to the glittery lights of Hong Kong. But now was not the time to play with such ideas.

My fingers trembled as I pulled open the slip of paper. The air was picking up around me—a storm was approaching—and I wondered if I should go back inside in case the wind carried off my precious paper. But I held it tight and squinted at the words:

Ming Hong,

How are you? It has been so many years. But the days and weeks here are all the same, blending together like a big soup, so in some ways, it's like no time has passed at all. Isn't that funny to think about?

I still remember the night we spent at your house by the sea. Maybe you've forgotten now because it was so long ago. I usually try to push away the bad

memories from that time-there are so many of them-
but that memory always makes me smile. I remember
you were very careful with the sweet potato that I'd
brought and how you lit the fire. I had never seen my
father use the woodstove, but you looked like you
knew what you were doing. Did you help your mother
at home before?

I hope you liked the sweet potatoes I left you. I still
grow some in a little patch of garden, hidden away
behind the back of the house where my aunt won't find
it. If she knew, she'd take everything for herself. She
always does.

My father died after I went home, and my aunt took
over the household. She works me very hard. I am always
cooking and cleaning. She hovers around me like a
mosquito looking for another bite, another reason for
me to be in trouble.

I don't know why I am writing this to you in a
letter except that it makes me feel free. I can say
what I want to and not worry about what my aunt
or the other girls will think. Writing this, it's as if
I've grown wings, like I can soar above the village and
watch everything from up high and never have any
of its dirtiness touch me. Do you ever have that
feeling?

I don't know if I will ever have the chance to give this to you. But even if your eyes never see them, at least I know that the words are written.

May the path ahead be always steady,

Fei

I read and reread the letter, my eyes straining in the dim light. The moon was hidden behind the storm clouds, but still I read her words until they were burned into my mind. I was smiling so wide, I thought my cheeks would burst. Fei remembered me. She thought of me, and often. Her words touched a part of me that I didn't remember existed. It wasn't just that I was happy.

I was hopeful.

The first clap of thunder jolted me back to reality. The skies opened, and sheets of rain tumbled down. I tucked Fei's letter into my shirt and hunched over to protect it as I sprinted back to the dorm. I collapsed inside, sodden. The other boys were preparing for bed, their curious eyes following me. Li was back, and he gave me a little knowing wink.

"Hey, what are you so happy about?" Tian asked with a smirk. "You meet one of those sexy fox spirits out there? She put you under a spell?"

I was grinning like an idiot. And I didn't care that he was

teasing me. I whooped and dove for Tian and wrestled him to the ground. The other boys cheered us on until I held Tian in a headlock.

"All right, all right," Tian conceded. He rubbed the back of his neck. "Beating up Li this morning, and now me? You're becoming a regular animal."

I smiled and let him go. I had never beaten Tian in a grappling match before.

When everyone was in bed, I waited until I could hear soft snoring before I pulled out Fei's letter again. It was a little damp from the rain, but the ink hadn't run, and I was careful as I straightened it out over my knees. Her words brought a smile to my face again. By now, I pretty much knew the letter by heart, but I still wanted to see the fine lines of her neat hand. I tucked the letter under my pillow and closed my eyes, imagining her hunched over the letter as she wrote. To me.

My mind danced with the tangled fragments of poetry and phrases that would make up my reply.

PART II

破四旧立四新

Destroy the Four Olds,
Support the Four News

WINTER, 1968

七

CHAPTER 7

LI

I didn't want to read the letter. The business between a man and a woman—that's a private affair. At least, that's how it was in the city. I mean, you wouldn't see courting girls and boys holding hands or doing anything except *talking* in public. But as long as their actions were not untoward, it was nobody else's business.

But in the village, I realized, it was *everybody's* business.

I still couldn't believe Ming hadn't spoken to the girl in six years—*six years*. I'd asked Fei about it, and she had laughed, scarlet rising to her pretty face. "That's not what happens here," she'd said. "It's not like the city."

I just shook my head. I had barely been there two weeks then, and I had already heard the comparison more times than I could count. The villagers all seemed to think that life in Guangzhou, "the city," was almost magical. They had asked me over and over again to describe indoor plumbing and toilets. Few of them had ever been more than ten miles from the place they were born. It was difficult to obtain permission to travel on non-Party business, even if one was just visiting family.

There were other things about the village that I didn't understand. The first day, I'd been hoping to wash off the sweat and dirt of work and remembered seeing a river on our drive in. So I'd asked Wang about it, but he just shook his head.

"You can't go to the river," he said.

"Aww, don't worry—I won't go in deep or anything." I wasn't a strong swimmer, but I was pretty sure I'd be okay to dip my toes in and rinse off.

"No one can go. It's haunted," Wang said.

"Haunted? What do you mean, it's haunted?" But Wang just shrugged and went back to his cards.

"You can go to the beach," Tian finally offered. "The water is salty, but Ming loves it. He's probably there now."

I nodded my thanks, and he gave me some vague directions. That was the night I first swam with Ming.

No one would tell me anything else about the river. "It's haunted," Ming said when I asked him, and he gave me the same shrug as Wang.

I wanted to make a comment, push him for an answer, but the pained expression on his face told me there was something else there—that it wasn't just another silly village superstition.

So I didn't ask.

When it came to superstitions, the villagers had loads. One insisted his illiteracy brought him good luck. "The word *book* sounds like *lose*, so I stay away. Better for mah-jongg," he tutted when he spotted us hunched over our texts.

There was the old lady in town who "read faces." She claimed to be able to tell if you would be lucky and have a good life.

"Your lobes are big like the Buddha," she told Feng. "You will have good fortune and great success; it is in the stars."

"Nonsense, my success comes from hard work and discipline. I thought these superstitions and counterrevolutionary beliefs had been purged from China," Feng had scoffed.

"It's pretty harmless." I actually found it kind of charming, but I didn't say that.

"She'd be arrested if she was in Guangzhou." The way he spoke, I wondered if he had half a mind to march the old lady to the labor camps himself.

The old lady cackled as if reading my mind and turned to me. "You, you have a handsome face. You have a cleft in the chin. It means you seek attention," she went on. I frowned, unsure of how to answer that, but she didn't stop for my opinion. "But I also think it means something else. The angle of your nose says the same. Long and strong. You will lead two lives."

Her words chilled me. It was utter nonsense, silly folklore, but the way her eyes bored into me, I couldn't help but wonder what she saw.

Feng shook his head beside me. "Of course you say that about us. We have already had two lives, first under the brainwashed bourgeois and now rebirthed as Chairman Mao's people." He chuckled. "Honestly, you villagers are ridiculous. You see a rat and think it's a demon."

Feng's practicality brought some comfort, but I couldn't shake the creeping sensation.

A double life.

I knew somehow that Feng was wrong. The old lady meant another life, different from the one I'd led up to now. For a moment, I wondered if she meant a life outside China, one where I wasn't working for the glory of the Party.

Even thinking it was counterrevolutionary, and I dismissed the idea as soon as it came to mind.

But it didn't stop my heart from racing.

Ming and I spent our evenings at the beach. After that first night, I stayed out of the surf, sticking to the protected cove. I was getting much better at swimming. Ming was a patient instructor and an exceptional swimmer. In the water, his shyness was gone. He was confident and sure, each stroke deliberate. There was no doubt in my mind that Ming was a demon of the sea.

I was waiting for him one evening, gazing out at where the sky joined the water. The lapping of the waves was hypnotic, and I felt my mind empty. Village life was far from easy, but its challenges could be a welcome distraction.

Ming hurried toward me, a piece of paper clutched in his hand. The eager look on his face told me there would be no swimming today. "You finished?" I asked.

He nodded. "I—I was hoping—I was wondering..." he stammered, his face red as a gourd, his hand shaking as he held out the page. "Could you . . . read it?"

I bit my lip, not sure how to respond. Ming and I had become close, but we had only known each other a few months. Except for Tian, who acted like his older brother, Ming didn't seem to have many friends. He was more than an orphan; he was an outcast in this tiny community where everyone was everyone else's minder. I couldn't help feeling sorry for him.

"Are you sure you want me to?" I asked. "It's very . . . personal."

Ming nodded. "You're a words man. I need you to tell me if it's good."

I took the letter from him and unfolded it. He'd been working on it for weeks, so I was expecting a lengthy exposition or even a well-crafted poem. But Ming's letter amounted to no more than a couple of paragraphs.

Comrade Fei,

How are you? I am fulsome and in good health. I was surprised to receive your letter of communications. It was acceptable to me.

I, too, recall that day that you wrote of. The weather had been pleasing for the season. The sweet potatoes were satisfying and sufficient. I am obliged to recompense your esteem.

It is of the utmost importance to arouse the broad masses of women to join in productive activity. I am pleased that you are productive with the matters that are of concern to you about your aunt.

"Comrades throughout the Party must never forget this experience for which we have paid in blood."

Women hold up half the sky, and I thank you for your words and diligent service.

Ming

I bit my lip to keep from laughing. What *was* this? I stole a quick glance at Ming, who was eyeing me carefully.

"Well, what do you think?"

"Um, did you . . . did you use Mao quotes?"

Ming blushed. "I wasn't sure what to write. I copied them because they looked good. And, well . . ." He hung his head. "I don't really know anything about women."

I heaved a sigh and reached over to lay a hand on his shoulder. "Believe it or not, they're just like us. Just . . . softer, maybe." To be honest, I didn't have the first clue about women either, but I was pretty sure this letter was a disaster.

"She's never going to like me," Ming moaned, collapsing on the sand beside me. "What was I thinking? There's no hope."

I clapped him on the back, filled with brotherly affection. "Of course there's hope. She wrote to you first," I reminded him. "What did she say in her letter?"

"She talked about her family. And the time she and I . . . well, we . . ." His voice trailed off, and he laid his forearm across his eyes. "You must think I'm such a fool."

"Nonsense, I don't think that at all. But I do think you're going to have to sharpen up this letter if you don't want to look like one."

Ming pulled his arm away enough so he could peer up at me. "I wrote something else." His voice was muffled, but I could just make out the words. "But I thought it was stupid."

"Show me." It had to be better than what I was holding.

Ming was quiet for a while, his eyes on the waves while he searched his mind. When he spoke, the words were strong and sure, like his strokes in the water.

> *I see*
> *the glittery sparkle of your shores.*
> *I listen*
> *to the spirit of the words that fall from your lips.*
> *I taste*
> *the salty sweetness of my tears as I suffer.*
> *I smell*

the stench of decay that I cannot rub from my being.
I yearn to touch
your beautiful wet sand, like soft, supple skin.
I ache to become
my true self that I can see through your eyes.

"That's beautiful." I didn't fully comprehend the intentions behind the words, but I knew they were true. There was something else. "It's not about Fei, is it?"

Ming shook his head. I knew this poem was laden with dangerous secrets that I normally would have buried, for Ming's sake as well as my own. Its very existence was counter-revolutionary. But my curiosity got the better of me. Here, with the ocean's murmuring to drown out our fears, it felt like we could be alone with our true thoughts.

I hazarded a guess. "Is it . . . is it about your father?" Ming was tight-lipped about his past, but I had overheard some of the villagers whispering.

"It's about Hong Kong." Ming's voice was so low I could barely hear it. Those words were laden with danger and promise. "My father dreamed of going there. He said, 'The ocean is a powerful force that can carry your hopes or crush your qi.'" He stopped, but I knew that wasn't the whole story. I knew I shouldn't press, but I couldn't let it go.

"Your father was escaping to Hong Kong." I'd heard about

people who had tried this, escapees who had been captured along the shores of the peninsula, sent to labor camps, condemned, and denounced for their betrayal. In a village like this, it would have marked Ming and his family as undesirables, fan ge ming who had to be persecuted for their crimes.

"It was during the famine, the Three Years of Natural Disasters. We knew he'd dreamed of it; we could see it in his eyes even when Ma wouldn't let him talk about it. He told me in secret how he would do it, how I could join him. Ma never believed it. She always thought he wouldn't, that he couldn't leave us behind, but I guess she was wrong."

Despite my earlier curiosity, I felt rage bubbling deep within me. How could this reactionary abandon not only the Party but also his family? But I didn't want to upset Ming, and I set aside my emotions to listen to my friend. "Why do you think he left?" I asked.

Ming considered this. I didn't think anyone had asked him before. "It was . . . different then. Times were hard, and we did what we could to—to survive." His face was stony, his mouth twisted with regret as he continued. "My father said he had a cousin there. Uncle Po would give him a job, and he would send us money. That was the plan. To help our family. He said I could join him when I was older."

He looked out to the sea. "He left in the middle of the night after the first harvest. Didn't say goodbye. When Ma woke up, she knew. She was furious at him, but I was . . . I was secretly pleased."

I was fascinated, in awe of Ming's belief in his father. It was so naive, but part of me was jealous that this village boy could have big dreams that didn't involve the Party or any of Mao's teachings. It left me feeling empty inside. What did *I* want?

"What happened to him?"

Ming bowed his head. "He didn't . . . he didn't make it. We got a letter from Uncle Po. He never registered. He never set foot in Hong Kong. A few days later, his body washed back up on shore. Ma wouldn't let me see it. He had been shot by the guards and left to drown. He died at sea."

I had one more question, but it was too dangerous to consider.

Do you still want to go?

I was pretty certain I already knew the answer.

★ ★ ★

"What were you two doing out there?"

We'd almost reached the dormitory when the voice came over the crunch of gravel beneath our bare feet. I hadn't bothered with shoes for weeks now. It was remarkable how quickly we were all losing the marks of our urban upbringings and becoming the hardworking peasants we were supposed to aspire to be.

Ming blushed, as though Feng would be able to read the conversation we'd had on our faces.

"Comrade Ming has been teaching me to swim," I said evenly.

Feng snorted. "Swimming? I didn't realize comrades had time for such leisurely activities."

"How can you say such a thing?" I cried in mock horror. "What about the Great Chairman's swim in the Yangtze? All my life, I have felt severely lacking because I didn't have this discipline, and now my dear comrade is granting me this gift." I gave Ming a wink. "And I must say, I have never before heard anyone use Mao quotations so ingeniously; he recites them to make sure my strokes are in rhythm."

Feng snorted again. "I'm pleased to hear Comrade Ming is studying hard, but reciting Chairman Mao's words means nothing if he does not live truly and wholly by their intentions."

I was taken aback by Feng's irritable mood. Since that first night when he and Tian had exchanged verbal blows that almost became physical, he'd become more withdrawn and sullen, quick to point out others' flaws, especially when it came to their outward devotion to Mao's teachings. He'd never used such retorts before. I wondered if he disapproved or was even jealous of my friendship with Ming.

Embarrassed, Ming mumbled a hasty reply, but Feng ignored

him. "Squad Leader wants to see you," he said to me as I went inside to drop my towel on my bed.

I noticed the small bundle of papers on his bunk. "Is that mail?"

Feng only grunted in reply. I took off to find the commander.

Most of the other city boys were living in groups in abandoned houses in the villages; only the four of us were staying with local boys. Our comrades had called us heong haa zai—country hicks—when they'd first made the assignments, but they had eventually realized that we all actually *liked* the locals. Well, with the possible exception of Feng, as I recalled his snappish attitude toward Ming.

I picked my way through the village toward the small house where the commander was living with three other youths. I entered without bothering to knock. "How are you, comrades?" I called out to the room.

"Oi, pretty boy," a boy named Qiang called out. "You ready to lose your coupons this week? Join in." A lot of the boys seemed to have picked up gambling to pass the time.

I smiled and shook my head. "Maybe next time, Qiang zai," I said, calling him by his nickname. He winked and went back to his cards. "Where's Hongbing? Feng said he was looking for me. Is there mail?"

There was a soft thud as a pair of worn boots landed beside me. "Comrade Li," Hongbing said, jerking his head toward his bunk, made with military precision. Hongbing was more muscular than the rest of us, and with his sleeveless shirt and buzz cut, he looked a bit like a Western soldier. Hongbing was the leader of our Communist Youth League, partly due to his fervent political activity and partly thanks to his father's position in the Guangzhou Cabinet Ministry.

"The village life treating you rough, comrade? You're tan as an African." Hongbing sifted through the piles of letters on his bunk. His fingernails were neatly trimmed and clean, while mine were still crusty with mud.

"Well, it's taken some adjusting, but it's important to make the most of our time here," I said carefully. "You know, for the cause." I always watched my words around the commander and the other senior officers, because you never knew when something could be misconstrued and counted against you.

Hongbing pulled a tan envelope from his satchel and waved it at me. "You're a good worker, Li, and a dedicated comrade. I've had my eye on you. If you keep this up, maybe we can make a request for you to be promoted to second-in-command. It'll put you in good stead for your future in the Party."

My eyebrows shot up. *Second-in-command?* "Really, Commander Hongbing, that would be . . . that would be a great honor." I kept my voice even, not finding it hard to muster the enthusiasm and humble pride he would expect. The conversation with Ming on the beach seemed like it had happened to someone else. I had a future in the Party; how could I even consider abandoning the cause?

I took the letter, and Hongbing gave a little grunt. He straightened up, although even at his full height, he barely came up to my shoulders. I resisted the urge to salute.

"Haiyo! Sik si laa nei!" It sounded like Qiang zai was cleaning up in the card game. There was a chorus of moans as the boys reached into their pockets and dug out the scraps of paper they were using to keep score. Even with the commander keeping a close eye on things, I wondered if there were actual coupons or even money on the line.

"Come on, Li," Qiang zai called out to me again. "You're missing out!"

I shook my head and flashed him a smile. "I couldn't deprive you of the fun."

Qiang zai chuckled and scooped together his winnings.

The air was cooler, less sticky than it had been since we'd arrived. Summer was finally over, and I wondered what winter had in store for us. Guangzhou had relatively mild winters, and I'd been told to expect the same here with the added balminess from the open sea. Maybe Ming and I could continue our nightly swims.

The envelope in my hands was crinkled at the corners where it had been shoved into a mailbag and thrown on the back of a truck. I recognized my father's beautiful neat hand, the strokes of his letters coming together like a painting.

I ripped open the flap, smiling as I unfolded the many sheets of paper. My father was expressive, full of ideas and musings, and not known for brevity.

My son,

It is pleasing to hear you are well and that life in the countryside suits you. You and your comrades are doing important work for the Party and the country of China-you must apply the same dedication and commitment to your work there as you did to your studies, in particular the field of mathematics.

I smiled at my father's dry wit, even on paper. He knew very well that math had never been my strong suit. I was much more inclined toward literature and the arts. A wave of longing to be with my family passed through me.

Your mother and I are well, as are your sister and brother. I must apologize that it has taken me a while to write back to you. The city council has chosen my team to oversee the planning for our section's new plumbing infrastructure. It is a great honor to be leading such an important project as government sewage.

I smiled again as my father went on to talk about my family. Mother was well, tending the household and working on her embroidery. I pictured her nimble fingers flying over the lines of gold thread. Her stitches were neat and tight; she accepted nothing less than perfection. I wished Father had described what she was working on so I could imagine the beautiful birds or dainty flowers meticulously stitched onto crisp white handkerchiefs.

My brother, Tze, had started working at a garment factory. A pang of guilt went through me as I read about how he was steaming Party uniforms and ladies' undergarments. Shy and quieter than I was, Tze should have been taking the university exam this year, just a year behind me. But since the Red Guards had taken over, entrance exams had been canceled. Somehow, as I'd stood beside my comrades, chanting the slogans and waving banners, I'd never really considered what people like my brother would do if they had nowhere to go to school.

Of course, as a good Communist, it was better to be doing honest labor than being corrupted by the institution.

I pushed aside thoughts of gentle Tze puffing and sweating in a haze of steam and read about my sister. Little Pearl, the jewel of our family, beloved by all. She was pretty, smart, and had a quick mouth, just like my father. We knew that out of all of us, she was the one destined for greatness. She had been chosen when she was only ten to join the Young Pioneers movement and had impressive political and career aspirations. When we were in school, she had outshone me despite being three years my junior. She was on the basketball team and the school newspaper. My parents could not be prouder, although Father sometimes joked that his only desire was to marry Pearl off to a wealthy old businessman. She always pouted, even though she knew he was teasing. At the start of the Cultural Revolution, Pearl had been selected for the Little Red Guards straightaway. Unsurprisingly, Father wrote, Pearl was now writing revolutionary articles for the Little Red Guard magazine.

She says she deeply misses her favorite brother, though she is pleased you are doing the good work of the Party.

I blinked away the threat of tears and hoped that the university exams would be reinstated in time for her to sit for them.

Stay strong and true, my son, and never forget your great purpose to the Party and the benevolent leader.

I reread Father's letter three times, soaking in every word, every description. Being so far from my family had felt like a constant emptiness in my bones.

I feared for my brother's and sister's futures. They were working, carrying out their duties to the country the same as I was, but they should have been at university, pursuing their own dreams instead of the Party's causes. I couldn't silence the niggling voice in my head. *All this for what?*

I strode back toward the dormitory, trying to will away the heaviness in my heart. I thought of the goodness of the people, Mao's strong face, and his bold visions of the future. But the little voice asked again:

All this for what?

八

CHAPTER 8

LI

My palms were sticky despite the cool weather. I ran them down my pants legs, feeling Ming's letter crinkling in my pocket. I sucked in a breath before rapping on the door.

Fei swung the door open, a laundry basket resting on her hip and a rag tied tightly around her head. A strand of hair had escaped, curling over her forehead. I could see why Ming was so smitten with the girl. She smiled brightly and ushered me inside.

Last week, Hongbing had called the newly rusticated youths together to discuss an educational exchange program. "The villagers have been very generous and patient in teaching us the traditions of farming and agriculture; we are doing the honest work of the people," Hongbing had declared, gesturing as though addressing eager masses and not thirty bored boys. "We want to repay our debt by sharing what we, as Chairman Mao's educated youth, have that is of greatest value and importance: the teachings of our benevolent leader, Chairman Mao Zedong."

There was a groan behind me. "It is through his teachings that we may all become better comrades and better serve the Party and its mission. But our village brethren—while they have been working hard to serve the Party in their own right, for which my comrades and I are grateful—have had to make the ultimate sacrifice when it comes to education."

He bowed his head respectfully.

"But today," he boomed, lifting his chin, "the Cadre and I are happy to announce a new program, through which we will share our gifts in the true Communist spirit. Starting tomorrow, the city youths will visit homes here and in nearby villages to dispense the wisdom of Chairman Mao's teachings and help local families fully comprehend the impact of his words so that all may understand their truth."

"*Hou ye!*" When they had made this announcement to the villagers and townsfolk, the Cadre and the other Party officials had burst into wild applause, raising their hands above their heads and nodding to the crowd. Slowly, a scattering of unenthused clapping rose. Something told me this was not the first time they had sat through one of these self-important speeches.

So that was how I found myself standing in the Shu house in Long-chi, clutching my well-worn copy of Mao's Red Book. I was aware of Ming's letter and kept fiddling with a frayed thread just above my pocket. Inspired by his poem, Ming and I had worked together on another verse that was dedicated to Fei's beauty and kind heart. We both hoped she would like it.

Fei set the laundry down by the door before closing it behind me. "Please come in," she said, gesturing to a wooden stool, the only place to sit in the sparsely furnished room. The one room was used for eating, sleeping, and receiving guests, while the cooking was done out back in a little alcove similar to the one we had in the dorm. "Pardon the mess," she said, ducking her head. "Aunt Shu, the tutor is here."

I glanced toward the kitchen alcove, where an older woman who must have been her aunt was busying herself over a pot. She had a hand over her mouth and nose and was desperately fanning the flames beneath the brick stove. Thick black smoke snaked out of the vents and stretched through the room.

"Aiyo, Ah Fei!" She coughed the name with contempt. "The wood is too wet! How many times do I have to tell you, ben dan?" *Stupid egg.*

Fei flushed, her cheeks turning a pale shade of pink that reminded me of cherry blossoms. She didn't say a word but knelt down to take over the fanning of the flames. She coughed as tendrils of smoke wrapped around her.

Finally, the fire properly contained, Aunt Shu stepped away from the stove and turned to me. She too sported a headdress made from an old rag, though I could see little wisps of gray hair poking out the sides. Her eyes were severe, her mouth turned down so I could count the wrinkles around it. She wiped her fingers on a towel draped over her shoulder and tramped over to me, her thick callused feet falling like ox hooves.

I jumped when she brought the towel down like a whip, the worn cloth striking the floor with a loud crack. "So, Cadre thinks you know more than us?" she barked. "You have something to teach me, eh? Do your words feed hungry mouths? Who's going to come and cook while I sit and listen to your yammering?"

It was my turn to look at the floor with embarrassment, my cheeks uncomfortably hot.

I kept my eyes down and chose my words carefully. "Of course, ma'am, Chairman Mao recognizes the hard work of women, especially when it comes to running a home." I glanced quickly at Fei, trying to remember what she had told me about her aunt. "Your husband passed away and left you on your own. Before, a woman without a husband was considered nothing, her family cast aside by the community. But I can tell, Shu tai, that this has not been the case for you. You are strong, tireless, and brave." I dared to lift my head and meet her gaze.

"It is Chairman Mao who tells the women of today to lift up their heads and be seen as equals," I continued, my voice steady. "The days of feudal patriarchy are over, and women will stand on equal footing in the future."

Aunt Shu tilted her head, considering my words.

Finally, she nodded, the corners of her mouth turning slightly upward. I sighed in relief, and Fei hurried to retrieve a couple of upturned wooden buckets to use as makeshift chairs.

Fei was a fast learner, quickly grasping ideas and concepts and even offering interpretations of her own. Aunt Shu was slower, and she refused to do anything except memorize the sayings by rote. I encouraged her to make her own connections, but she only frowned and repeated the phrases. She managed to recall two short quotes by the end of our session, while Fei committed to heart a whole passage on art and culture.

The sun was starting to set by the time we finished and the steamy smell of soup permeated the air. A thundering of feet and laughter approached the house. I stood up, and Aunt Shu went to tend to her cooking as three grubby-looking boys stormed in.

"Hey, who's that?" a young boy of about ten shouted, pointing at me. "He looks like Wu Suxin!"

"It's rude to point, Ru," Fei scolded gently, ruffling the boy's hair. "Go wash your hands for dinner." The boys hollered and pushed their way to the washbasin in the corner.

"He just loves the old movie stars." Fei turned away, trying to hide her pink face. I nodded and resisted the urge to smile. I was familiar with Wu Suxin, especially what the girls thought of his good looks!

There was a loud metallic clatter. "Wah!" Aunt Shu hissed in pain, sucking on her finger, where the lid of the pot had burned her. The boys were shouting and playfully shoving one another while they washed up.

I felt another pang of sadness. The delicious smells of cooking, the laughter of the boys—it reminded me of home.

Fei must have sensed my sorrow. "Would you like to stay for dinner?" she asked softly. Out of the corner of my eye, I saw Aunt Shu wheel around to glare at her niece.

I swallowed and shook my head. "That's very kind, but there wouldn't be enough."

"Of course there's enough!" Aunt Shu snapped, though I sensed they were just words of pride. Sure enough, as she ladled up a bowl, I could hear her muttering under her breath. "The Cadre doesn't feed his own legion?"

"No, no, it's okay, Shu tai, I really couldn't. The other boys would be upset," I protested in an attempt to help her save face, even as she shoved the bowl under my nose. It took at least two more refusals before she huffed and continued to lay out bowls for the boys.

"Thank you for your teaching today," Fei said as she opened the door. I remembered—*the letter*. It was still in my pocket, the edges creased from how I'd been sitting.

"This is for you. No, not from me," I added quickly when I saw her eyes widen in confusion. "It's from Ming." I kept my voice to a whisper.

She gasped and met my gaze. Then her lips curled up into a delightful smile and without a word, she pocketed the letter and gave me a nod.

"Ah Fei!" Shu cut short our farewell. Fei smiled again, and I gave her a tiny bow as she shut the door.

As I strode back up the alleyway, I whistled a little tune. "Greensleeves," an English folk song, one of my father's favorites before the Revolution. I don't know what came over me. Back home, I would never have dared to even hum the first few notes, but I suddenly had to hear it. I did a step-hop to match the crescendo, my heels clicking to keep the rhythm. Soon I was bouncing and then skipping along, the music still building in my bones. I belted out the notes, my voice warbling, the way I remembered my father playing it on the *pipa*. Nearby, a door opened, and a confused face poked out. I winked at my curious audience but didn't stop. Seeing Fei's delight in Ming's letter, I'd felt a lightness I hadn't had in a long while, since even before I'd arrived in the village. When I was almost at the dormitory, I recognized what it was.

A sense of purpose.

★ ★ ★

The days were getting shorter as winter approached, but the work in the fields never slowed down. We were deep into harvesting the autumn and winter crops, large fields of millet and some smaller plots of peanuts. While the rest of the village harvested the winter wheat and millet crops, we were put to work breaking up the soil to get the fields ready for spring planting.

Our backs were stiff from sleeping on the wooden slats and

coarse straw mats of the bunk beds that had been brought in for us. We had all brought our own bedrolls from the city, but these had quickly taken on a musky odor that filled the room, so we had been issued rations of fabric to construct thin blankets. A room full of boys our age who worked all day and rarely bathed meant body odor was rampant.

Every morning after a meager breakfast, we registered at the work hall and then headed out to the fields, where we worked on our assigned sections. Unlike most of the villagers, who kept their own tools at home, we were given communal tools—rusty picks and blunt shovels that probably hadn't been cared for since the Great Leap Forward.

We had graduated from the single sweet potato field we had all worked on when we'd first arrived in the village. While one or two villagers might look after an entire field on their own, we city boys were given smaller patches to work on, and for good reason. Every time I wielded my pickax, I was convinced I was going to strike my own feet. The ground was hard and stubborn, and it felt like we were chipping at marble. How were we supposed to turn this into fertile earth?

"Put your backs into it!" the older villagers shouted as they patrolled our line. Zhu sifu, as he demanded we call him, had formally retired but had been brought back to train us fledgling farmers. Anytime one of us stopped for a rest, Zhu sifu barked in our faces. "You entitled little snots! My grandmother could hoe better than you!" He was already toothless, so his scolding peppered our necks and faces with spittle.

During our midday break, we stumbled back to the dormitory for a quick lunch, usually plain noodles with bland broth. We rested, wrote letters home to our families, and dreamed about the letters we would write to the girls we knew if it wasn't considered inappropriate.

After a long afternoon of work, we finally finished up for the day when it was too dark to see the ground before us. We reported to the village accountant to receive our work points for the day. We were always the last team to be counted, and our points were measly compared to the villagers' scores, even the women.

Every night, we prepared our meals in the cramped little alcove. We had cooked for one another a few times, but most of the time the village boys prepared their own meal and we looked after ourselves. I had never been a fussy eater, but I had to choke down my meals; none of us were particularly good cooks. Our rations were tied to our work points, and despite our best efforts, we were falling behind on our quota, and food was getting scant. After the first month, most of us had to ask our families to send supplies.

Gradually, we started improving. Zhu sifu still shouted and cursed at us, but our daily points increased. My hands had blistered over more times than I could count, and smooth calluses were forming in the spots where I gripped my tools, providing a welcome cushion. My muscles had hardened, the skin tightening over new sinew.

I was becoming a peasant.

One late-autumn afternoon, Zhu sifu was patrolling the lines, shouting and spitting as usual. His voice took on a feverish pitch as he bellowed. "Move along, you lazybones, work faster! My ancient hands can pick ten times faster than the lot of you." He stooped over Feng and spat against his ear. "What's wrong, worm nut? You don't like an old man shouting at you?"

Feng said nothing, which seemed to infuriate Zhu sifu even more. "You think you're better than me with your school smarts and city mannerisms? You think you know things? You don't know anything!" Feng was doing his best not to squirm under the abuse, his fingers tightening around a tangle of roots he was trying to pull up.

Zhu sifu was getting worked up, more so than usual. Feng's indifference was frustrating him. Suddenly, the old man straightened up, glaring at all of us. "You lot are nothing but a bunch of spoiled, whining layabouts. Spewing your damn speeches and fancy quotes about Communism and sticking up big-character posters. You call that revolution? We peasants, we're the ones who have suffered. You city folk whined about the tough times when your cigarettes were rationed while we ate nothing but bark and weeds. You call that reform?"

The whole brigade had stopped working, and we eyed one another nervously. The old man was speaking against the Party and its fundamental ideologies. In the city, any one of us would have jumped in to put an end to this tirade. But here, what were the rules?

I set down my hoe and inched my way toward him. "Zhu sifu, maybe you should go inside. Have a bit of a rest," I said calmly.

"Rest? I haven't rested for ten years." His eyes were wild as he whipped around to face me. "Every time I close my eyes, I see my children's sunken eyes begging me for food. My wife boiled dirt and bugs to have something to give them in their bowls. You want rest? How can you rest when you were too weak even to bury your own children?" He sank to his knees, clawing at bits of dirt.

"Zhu sifu, I'm . . . I'm sorry for your loss." The old man just sobbed, digging his fists into his eyes. I felt terrible.

"They were the hard years," Feng spat, clearly unmoved. "Natural disasters cursed our country, challenged our people. All of China suffered, but we rose up stronger."

Nobody else said a word. Some of the boys bowed their heads, avoiding Feng's eye.

"What is going on here?" a voice bellowed. Commander Hongbing was headed toward us, one of the other brigade leaders by his side.

"What is the meaning of this, Zhu? These boys are your responsibility," the brigade leader shouted. The old man replied with a whimper and a sob, curled on the ground.

"Get back to work!" Hongbing snapped his fingers and stomped his foot so hard that mud splashed up onto his pristine uniform. Even though most of us had now abandoned our former Red Guard dress, he still wore the red band on his left arm.

Grumbling, the boys turned back to the ground. I made Feng help me try to coax Zhu to his feet, but the old man wouldn't budge, just lay on the ground murmuring over and over, "Please forgive me, Yiling. Please forgive me, Guozi."

"Old man's lost his bloody mind. Get him out of here!" the brigade leader spat. I pressed my lips together as Feng and I each slid a hand under Zhu's arms. His head lolled to the side, and his legs dangled so we had to drag him across the fields back to his home.

His wife ushered us in and had us lay him down on the bed. "Shh, you're making a fool of yourself," she muttered as she tucked him in.

"Is he going to be okay?" I whispered.

"He's old. His mind is going. And the fields, the sun, they give him bad thoughts sometimes," she said simply, laying a cool towel on her husband's forehead.

"You better watch him," Feng cautioned. "With that rubbish he's saying about the Revolution, he'll be lucky if he's not thrown in jail or sent to the labor camps. Doesn't matter how old he is."

"He's not been well. Not since the Three Years of Natural Disasters. He tries to forget, but these days, all he sees is our sons' bodies floating down the river." She gazed into her husband's eyes, but they were blank and unseeing.

I swallowed the lump in my throat. "We'd better go." I turned away.

As we walked back to the fields, Zhu's words haunted me.

Feng was strangely quiet. His steps were purposeful, chin tilted high like he was marching, the model soldier.

A thought hit me.

"Oi, Li! What's the deal?" he demanded when I grabbed his arm.

"You're not going to say anything, are you?"

"What are you talking about?" He tried to pull away.

"Back at the house, you said Zhu would be lucky if he wasn't thrown in jail. You're not going to report him, are you?" When Feng remained silent, I knew that was exactly what was on his mind. "He's old and sick."

The boy avoided my gaze. "These villagers shouldn't get special treatment just because they act dumb and simple," he insisted, but I could hear a slight tremble in his voice. "Reactionary crimes must be punished."

I grasped at Feng's collar, bringing my face close to his so I could feel his breath. "He's lost his children, his family, and now he's losing his mind. What would happen to his wife?" I was practically shouting.

"Li, what's your problem?" Feng wrenched himself free. "It's just one incident. Nothing will happen unless he has a history of reactionary crimes or counterrevolutionary behavior. When did you become such a sympathizer?"

The tone of his voice made my hair stand on end.

"You better watch yourself." Feng straightened his shirt, eyeing me warily. "People are talking, you know—that you're not fulfilling your Party duty in spreading Mao's doctrine. That orphan kid? The girl? You're not here to make friends, comrade, you're here to learn. You don't want the brigade to get the wrong idea."

I quietly fumed as we headed back to the fields. Of course Feng would report our little exchange. He wouldn't hesitate to brand me as a reactionary sympathizer. A bad mark against me meant the Party could send me to the labor camps, or worse. I should have been more worried about my own standing rather than fretting over the fate of old Zhu.

But I couldn't ignore that tiny little voice that was getting louder by the day. When it came to thoughts about the Party, I wasn't fighting so hard to keep them quiet anymore.

九

CHAPTER 9

LI

I was surprised to receive a letter from Tze. My brother wasn't lazy, he was just very efficient. Why waste time writing when he could send along his regards via our father? And unlike me, Tze was good with numbers, not words.

So I was even more stunned to pull a thick stack of paper from the envelope Hongbing handed me. I would never have expected more than a single page. I sat down to read his detailed account of two old men waiting for the bus outside our building, how they were dressed, the snippets of conversation he could grasp about the unusual humidity. This was followed by meticulous observations of the frazzled housewife laden with grocery bags who kept getting up and looking for the bus that he knew was already running late by seven minutes. Tze then remarked that this was actually on time, considering the delays of the past few weeks.

I realized why my brother had written. He was bored.

He had lost his job; the garment factory had been shut down by the Party without warning or explanation, so there was nothing for him to do. Since the Cultural Revolution had begun, a large majority of the high schools and universities had been closed to encourage more young people to dedicate their time to the cause. It had been a liberation for us, thousands of girls and boys taking up armbands, waving our red books and chanting, always chanting, to promote the words and thinking of Mao. The bands, the books, the chanting: It had all given us this great sense of belonging and righteous purpose.

But now, with the Red Guards disbanded and so many of us moving to the countryside, the rallies were done. Most of the schools stayed closed, since there were no teachers to run them; most were probably afraid of taking up their old positions. As a result, many of the students, including my brother, were left to amuse themselves.

I felt sorry for Tze. As the second son, he was stuck in my shadow, and there was some bitterness in our brotherhood. Our parents were always berating him. "Get a job, join the Party!" Mother scolded him constantly, trying to coax him out of the house. It became a point of pride for him, his ability to resist their perpetual nagging.

Tze was quiet and socially awkward and had never been a fan of politics, so he would never sign up for the Party. I worried that without some political activity or commitment to the

Communist cause, he could be a target for criticism. I'd seen many of my classmates, Party members and nonmembers alike, forced to confess to reactionary crimes or selfish thoughts that were counterrevolutionary. They were then sentenced to hard labor at reform camps as punishment. It was important to at least keep up the appearance of devotion. Even this mundane letter could be twisted around, a sinister motive attached to his idle thoughts.

I wondered if maybe he should come out to the countryside and join me, but I knew that would be heartbreaking for our mother. Plus, I wasn't sure he would be suited for this life.

I tapped the letter against my chin, pondering my brother's predicament as I gazed out over the crashing surf. There were soft footsteps behind me—Ming. I turned and gave him a big smile.

"Hey." I noticed the piece of paper clutched in his hand. "That a new letter?"

Ming nodded and sat down beside me, holding the page delicately. I'd passed a similar page to him just a couple of days ago: Fei's response to his first letter. The entire walk back from her house, I'd been itching to read it, but I'd managed to resist. Ming's delighted face over the past two days had told me everything I needed to know.

I was surprised he'd written a reply so quickly after the weeks he'd spent agonizing over that first one.

He held out the letter to me, though I had to tug a little to release it from his grasp. I should have just put it in my pocket, but I was dying to know what it said. "Do you want me to read it?"

Ming tucked his bottom lip between his teeth, hesitating for a moment, then nodded.

The letter was short again, which made my heart sink, but then I started to read.

My friend and confidant Fei,

How are you? I was very happy to receive your letter – it gave me so much joy. My eyes follow the marks of your hand, and I want to reach out and close my fingers around yours. Perhaps that is too forward for me to say, but when I think about you, I cannot stop the flow of happy thoughts and pure joy in my head and heart.

I read about your family. Li also tells me that your life at home is hard. I can imagine the boys laughing as their mother chases after them and hear your aunt's harsh tones when she scolds you. I want to leap through the page and shout her down. To protect you from her anger, to light the fires of the stove and keep them burning so that you never have to stoop over the smoldering coals and shed hot tears again.

You are right to remark that I am shy. I don't want to be shy; I want to share my thoughts and words with you. I want to share my dreams and hopes and many jokes. I want to share my sweet potatoes and secrets. I want to be a better person for you. I will make an effort to smile more simply because you asked.

Our days begin and end with the rising and setting of the sun, east to west. But maybe there's more to the end of the day than just darkness. Maybe in the nightfall, we will find the true light.

I look forward to your next letter, Fei. I yearn for your companionship, even if it is just through a leaf of parchment. For me, that it is written by your hand is more than enough.

May the road be ever swift and flowing,

Ming

I wanted to whoop and holler and congratulate Ming on his poetic masterpiece, but no doubt that would have just caused him greater embarrassment.

So I punched him in the arm. "Good words," I said.

Ming still blushed.

Just as I was putting his letter away, I was hit by a bolt of inspiration and shoved the letter back at him.

"Hey, why don't you deliver the letter yourself?" I exclaimed.

"I—I can't . . . her aunt," Ming stammered. "She'd never let me near her." He didn't say the rest of the sentence—*because of my father.*

"That's only because you don't have any reason to be talking to her niece." I could feel my eyebrows leaping up with excitement. "But we can get you one. An official reason for you to see and speak with Fei."

Ming frowned. "How do you mean?"

"Leave it to me."

★ ★ ★

Ming wiped his palms on his frayed trousers for the umpteenth time. I didn't think it was worth pointing out the sheen of sweat on his forehead. At least he'd taken the time to run his fingers through his hair in a rushed comb.

The door swung open, and Fei's eyes were as wide as the full moon.

"M-m . . ." His name remained unsaid, hanging on the edge of her lips.

"Good evening, Miss Fei," I said in my most formal tone. "May I introduce Comrade Ming Hong, a local from Dingzai village." I flashed her a smile.

They gaped at each other: a startled rat and a newborn cat, unsure who was predator and who was prey.

"Ah, Li, you're here." Aunt Shu was tying a towel around her head when she spotted Ming next to me. Her eyes narrowed. "What is *he* doing here?"

Fei cast her eyes downward while Ming's ears went crimson. I steeled myself and put on a big smile.

"Shu tai, this is Ming from Dingzai village. He is my good friend and an excellent comrade." I stepped forward and gestured for Aunt Shu to take a seat on the corner stool. "Ming has been chosen by our brigade leader to help direct our education program for the villages. And because of your exemplary performance and display of Party ideals, your household has been given the honor of receiving the benefits of this new directive." I gave emphasis to the words *exemplary* and *performance* and considered pounding my fist into my hand like I'd seen the great orators do during their speeches, but that might have been too much for the tiny room we were in.

It actually hadn't been difficult to convince Hongbing to let Ming come to my lessons with Fei and Aunt Shu. I threw around some quotes about the need for the peasants to take a dominant position in the new socialist transformation. "And what better embodiment do we have than this poor orphan who has lost everything but still stands proud, ready to further the cause of the Party?"

I don't think Hongbing really cared either way, and he granted his permission with a wave.

So now I was selling this to Aunt Shu with all the passion and charm I could muster.

Aunt Shu glared at Ming but gave a nod. Fei let out a little gasp of relief that she concealed with a light cough. Ming wouldn't look up, keeping his eyes on the ground as he took a seat beside Fei on the dirt floor.

I remained standing while Fei and her aunt pulled out their copies of Mao's quotations. "Today, we will look at Contradictions Among the People," I began. The women dutifully opened their copies. Ming glanced around awkwardly, and I realized he'd left his book at home. *So much for coming under the guise of being a teacher.* Fei noticed and leaned over to share her book with Ming.

"*Ahem.*" Aunt Shu made her opinion clear. The pair scooted apart, and Ming returned his gaze to the ground.

I found it hard to concentrate as we went over Mao's thoughts on indecision and conflict within the socialist sects. I tried to maintain the serious demeanor of a Party educator, but all the while, I was watching every flinch and gesture between Ming and Fei. At first, their arms were stiff by their sides. But as the lesson went on, I noticed that Fei's elbow seemed to nudge Ming's. Aunt Shu didn't notice, and Fei flinched back immediately, blushing and increasing the distance between them farther still. I suppressed a grin.

"Aiyo," Aunt Shu exclaimed midway through a passage. "Teacher, if you can't even read the words on the page, how are we simple peasants expected to follow?" she scolded.

"Forgive me, Shu tai. My head is not clear today." And I had a thought. "But now might be a good time for my assistant to relieve me while I collect myself."

Ming's head snapped up. I offered him my book. This was a passage we had gone over a few times together, so I hoped he'd be confident with it.

Fingers trembling, Ming took the book from my hands. It took him a while to find the right spot, and Fei managed to very quickly point it out before withdrawing her hand under the hawkeyed glare of her aunt.

"In order to build a great socialist society, it is of the utmost importance to arouse the broad masses of women to join in productive activity." I flinched as Ming's voice cracked and squeaked. But it grew in confidence as he went on. "Men and women must receive equal pay for equal work in production. Genuine equality between the sexes can only be realized in the process of socialist transformation of society as a whole."

"Well said, Ming." I applauded as if the words were his own. Ming stood up straighter and continued.

"China's women are a vast reserve of labor power. This reserve should be tapped in the struggle to build a great socialist country. Enable every woman who can work to take her place on the labor front, under the principle of equal pay for equal work. This should be done as quickly as possible." Ming made that final declaration with such uncharacteristic authority that I found myself slamming my hand to my chest as if swearing my unwavering allegiance.

He finished, shocked by his own performance. He looked to me for approval, and I flashed him a smile and a wink.

I wasn't the only one who approved. Fei was grinning from ear to ear, her eyes round, her cheeks a little pink with emotion. "I didn't know his words could be so wise," she murmured.

But most importantly, I had seen Aunt Shu swelling with pride. This hardworking peasant woman without a husband to support her was the quintessential female comrade Mao's words were intended for. While my motives might not have exclusively been in the interest of furthering socialism, the effect was profound.

Aunt Shu gave Ming a sidelong glance and a grunt. It wasn't approval, but it was certainly progress.

"Well, I think that wraps up today's lesson," I said. "We will take our leave."

Aunt Shu stood up and dusted off her trousers before heading straight for the stove, though not before setting her book down gently on the table. Fei leapt to her feet and showed us to the door.

Ming was still staring at the ground, but when he lifted his head to bid her good night, they exchanged a look of affection.

I hated to interrupt.

"Teacher Ming, maybe there's some homework you want to leave with your student?" I whispered, elbowing him in the ribs.

Ming's eyes lit up, and he fumbled in his shirt pocket. Fei's brow crinkled, and then her face smoothed into a shy smile when Ming withdrew a thin envelope.

"Ah, some reading for you," he said softly.

Fei gave a knowing tilt of her head and a little wave good night. I'd definitely say we'd made progress.

And that was more than enough for the night.

✝ CHAPTER 10

LI

I ventured into the surf, just up to my ankles. Ming was already out in the sea, oblivious to the cold. The chill cut so deep I could feel it in my bones. I was looking forward to the New Year and all it promised, though it would be the first time I would spend it away from my family.

Winter had been sullen and overcast, though up until now the water had been mild enough that Ming and I had kept up our swimming lessons. Meanwhile, fields still needed to be hoed and loosened, so the pace of our work hadn't slowed. Some of the educated youth had been put to work carving out channels for irrigation before the spring planting.

At night, we huddled in the darkness of the room lit by flickering lamps. I was surprised by the way the peasant boys were taking the study of Mao's words so seriously. Even Tian was writing and rewriting characters in the dust.

Hongbing was, of course, pleased to see their progress, and Feng took it upon himself to spend as much of his free time as possible reciting the words of Mao to our village brothers. He wasn't a great teacher, but no one could deny his passion.

"We should rid our ranks of all impotent thinking. All views that overestimate the strength of the enemy and underestimate the strength of the people are wrong."

"The prospects are bright, but the road has many twists and turns."

Of course, with the unfamiliar words, not to mention the way Feng delivered them, more than a few village boys were left scratching their heads.

"There was a foolish old man who had a house at the base of two mountains, but the mountains obstructed his view." Feng read a familiar story during one of our study nights. "So he set about moving a mountain with a pickax and shovel, one mound of earth at a time. A scholar passed the foolish old man and his sons toiling at the mountain and remarked on his foolishness. The foolish old man replied, 'If I do not complete this task, my sons will continue my work for me, and their sons after that. It will take many generations to chip away at our obstacles, but with enough time, we are sure to triumph.' The Buddha heard the old man's declaration and took kindly to his determination. The Buddha sent an angel to lift the mountains and remove them from the old man's view. And it was thus that the foolish old man accomplished the impossible."

Feng's smug grin was met with confused faces.

"Why didn't he just turn his house around?" Tian asked, his face disbelieving. "Who builds a house facing a mountain? What an idiot."

"That's not the point Chairman Mao is making," Feng sighed. "The lesson we can take from this allegory is that we must continue to strive for our ideals despite the odds. We must forever move toward the socialist transformation if it is to succeed."

"Sounds like a load of crap to me," Tian muttered, not trying to hide his contempt. "Like when the Cadre made us all melt iron pots for steel. Doing something stupid and calling it commitment to the cause is still stupid."

Feng squirmed uncomfortably and turned to me. I just shrugged. I'd never quite understood that story, even when I was a young Red Guard.

Unlike the Red Guards and the workers Mao had drawn into the Revolution in the cities, the peasants weren't shy about sharing their real opinions. Maybe it was because there was little danger of their thoughts being called "intellectual" or of them being accused of bourgeois behavior or being part of the landlord class. I found it all refreshing, the blunt common sense of it. While most of us in the Communist Youth Leagues had been falling over ourselves trying to prove how socialist we were in our thinking, the villagers didn't need to prove anything. The questions these boys asked, like the ones Fei and even Aunt Shu posed to me, were thought-provoking. Mao had always empha-sized the importance of self-criticism and examination, but I realized now that I'd never really seen those things practiced.

"Li!"

A cold splash against my knees snapped me back to the pres-ent. My rolled-up trousers were soaked, and the chill was becoming unbearable. Ming was waving wildly from the sea, pointing toward the rocks.

I followed his arm until a movement caught my eye. A figure was climbing the edge of a rocky outcrop, peering into the crashing surf. At first I thought it was a local fisherman, but he was too unsteady on his legs.

"Comrade!" I called out, starting back toward the beach to meet him. When he turned, I saw he was about my age, maybe a year or two younger. His hair was long, ruffling in the wind. He smiled and raised his hand in greeting but didn't move from the edge of the rocks.

I watched as he crouched down into a half squat, looking down into the water, like he was practicing tai chi.

Then he launched himself off the rock into a swan dive. Except he mistimed the jump, and he was left tumbling and flailing before landing on his back and being swallowed up by the sea.

"No!" I shouted as I watched the waves suck and push bru-tally against the rocks. I broke into a run, my feet slipping as I tried to hurry along the shore in my waterlogged clothes. I scrambled up the outcrop from which he'd leapt, hardly noticing the jagged rocks cutting into my callused feet. But by the time I reached the edge, there was nothing but white foam below.

After a long, awful moment, a dark mass of hair broke the surface, tossed about in the waves.

Ming was swimming desperately toward me, but he would never reach the boy in time. After only a moment's hesitation to shed my shirt and pants, I leapt off the edge.

The water was icy cold, and I regretted the jump immediately. But I shook off the biting sting as I kicked my way to the surface.

I fought the waves, swimming toward where I could just see the boy's hair bobbing on the surface, pushing away the image of my own head smashing against the rocks. I hauled my body through the water until I felt my fingers close around cold flesh.

The boy's awkward jump must have knocked him unconscious. He was a dead weight. With one arm wrapped around him and the other stroking steadily, I did my best to keep his head above the waves. My legs burned from the inside out, but I kept pushing toward the shore.

Ming reached us just as my feet found solid ground, and he wrapped his arms around the boy's legs. He was shorter up close and actually quite young, probably in his mid-teens. His skin was smooth, his body lean but not muscular, unlike the local youths. Together, we managed to carry the body and stumble back to the beach.

We collapsed in a wet heap, and I checked the boy's pulse. It was light but present, and I put my ear against his chest and heard short ragged breathing. I pounded his back once, twice, until a plume of water shot out of his mouth and dribbled out the sides. He coughed then, hacking and gasping. He tried to speak, and I bent closer to him.

"Did I make it? Am I in Hong Kong?" His whisper was barely audible. When I looked back at his face, he'd passed out again.

"We'd better get him to the nurse." Ming was already on his feet, dragging the boy by the armpits. I grasped him by the ankles and tried to stand, but my tired legs gave out under me, and I collapsed. Finally, I got to my feet, and we struggled through the village with our load.

By the time we left the boy with Nurse Xi and headed back to the dormitory, I was completely recovered.

"We saved a boy, Ming. We saved a comrade's life! What a glorious feat." I was bursting with excitement.

Ming was more subdued. "It was too dangerous. You could have died!"

"Are you kidding me?" I was beaming from ear to ear. "I feel amazing. I bet I could swim thirty *li* in the Yangtze river, just like Chairman Mao." I struck a gallant pose, waving to an imaginary crowd, like the newspaper photograph of the Chairman, clad in a simple robe after emerging from his historic ten-mile swim.

Ming stayed silent.

I was still full of energy when we returned to the dormitory, eager to recount our heroic tale to our comrades.

"Ming and I saw someone jump into the ocean," I said. "He jumped off the rocks, and I had to swim out to save him."

Tian frowned. "Impossible. Who's stupid enough to go swimming in winter?"

The comment stung, but I ignored my pride. "Tell them, Ming."

"It was a boy," he said quietly. "But I don't think he was a villager."

"Who was he? What was he doing out there?" Kamshui and Ah-Jun were both fascinated, but the village boys were quiet.

"That was the craziest part! He said he was—" But I was cut off by a sharp nudge from Ming.

"He was just—he was just going for a swim," Ming said hastily.

Tian lifted an eyebrow. "Going for a swim? Are you sure?" But he wasn't talking to me. He kept his gaze on Ming, coaching him with his eyes.

I opened my mouth to protest, but then I saw Ming's face. His lip was quivering, his eyes big and round. He didn't say anything.

Tian turned to me, his eyes narrowed. "Where'd you pull him out from?" he asked.

"Just down by the water. Off the cliffs," I said evenly.

Tian nodded and turned to the group. "Probably just a suicide then."

"A *suicide*?" I arched my brows. I hadn't thought that for an instant and was just about to say so.

"Yeah, it was probably just a suicide." Ming's voice was so timid, I hardly recognized it. I thought of protesting again, but Ming was now watching me with pleading eyes.

He was scared.

It was only then that I remembered what Ming had told me about his father. Was this what the boy was actually doing? Was he trying to escape to Hong Kong?

Even though I wanted to argue, I felt sorry for my friend, so I relented.

"Fine," I said. "I guess we just rescued a suicide jumper." I snatched my book of quotations and tried to read, but the words blurred together as I went over the rescue again and again in my head.

The rest of the evening was spent in tense silence.

★ ★ ★

The next evening, I collected a letter from home. There was a shiftiness in Hongbing's eyes when he handed me the thin envelope, bumpy along the edges like it had been opened and resealed.

"What's this?" I demanded, but Hongbing said nothing.

Back at the dormitory, I stuck my thumb under the edge, and the flap gave straightaway. Someone had opened my letter and not even bothered to cover their tracks. I felt a chill as I unfolded the sheet of paper and recognized my mother's minuscule handwriting.

My dearest eldest son,

Tragedy has befallen our family. Your father has been taken away. The guards came in, ransacked our books, destroyed our home, overturned everything. They confiscated some papers that your father had tucked away in a gap in the wall; I never knew they were there or what they were even about. And they took him away. They won't tell me anything, only that he has been sent to a prison camp in the southern region. They will not divulge his crimes or the charges against him, only that he must be suitably admonished for his reactionary thinking.

I am beside myself, a prisoner in my own house. I cannot go outside, for the neighbors whisper and cast judging glances. The shopkeepers won't serve me, and I hate to send Tze in my place. Your sister cannot show her face in the Youth League, and your brother still has no gainful employment; he will never find a job with this black mark on his record. Your father's actions have destroyed our family and cursed the Li name.

My son, my heart aches for you to return home. You

are fulfilling a duty to our great country, but it comes at the cost of your duty to your family. I shed a mother's bitter tears and wail for your return to care for your siblings.

Your heart-hurting mama

My heart stopped. My mind blanked. A cold nothingness settled over me.

There was no going back. Our family was doomed.

I don't know how many times I read my mother's letter, trying to make sense of the words. *My father in prison? A reactionary?* I pictured the gap in the wall. A part of the house had started to come apart with age, and Father was forever putting off fixing it despite Mother's constant nagging. Was this why? So he could use the crack as a hiding place to squirrel away incriminating documents? For how long? To what purpose? A mistake, surely, wasn't it?

A wave of nausea went through me, and I thought I would vomit, but only my thoughts kept churning.

★ ★ ★

The rest of the night was a blur. I walked. That's all I did. One foot in front of the other. I had no destination in mind. I may have been going in circles, naturally sticking to the familiar beaten paths.

I kept running over my mother's desperate plea in my mind. The suffering in her words pained me. She was fragile on her own; she relied wholly on my father financially and emotionally. I wanted to go home, but there was no way I would be allowed to leave. Besides, what reason could I give?

I need to go home because my father is in prison for being a counterrevolutionary.

It didn't make sense. It had to be a mistake, I told myself over and over. But there was a niggling hitch in my inner voice, a hesitation I couldn't deny.

What if it was true?

At some point, I'd wandered off those familiar paths, and now the ground was soft under my feet. I was trudging through mud and marsh, a long way from the village boundaries.

A gentle trickling came from up ahead, and something pulled me toward the sound. Now I was clambering over rocks, hunched over to feel my way along, my hands guiding my feet. It was too dark to see much, with thick trees blocking the moonlight. But I pushed on, ignoring the branches and the gravel cutting into my skin.

I don't know when I realized I'd reached the river—the haunted river the villagers had warned me about. I'd been wrong; I had been following a path, just one that was overgrown from lack of use. The wind picked up around me, and the branches cast gruesome shadows in the moonlight. Even though I knew it was nothing but a silly superstition, I was suddenly scared. My heartbeat pounded in my ears, drowning out the sound of rushing water.

And then a soft moan.

I whipped around, but there was nothing but black. My fingers clutched at the rocks. There was a rustling to my left, but once again, there was nothing there. I could feel my heart thundering.

I couldn't see him so much as feel him. A presence, suffocating every inch of my body down to the fine hairs on my arms and the spaces between my bones. And then there was a sudden flickering, like someone switching on a light in my mind, as the moon emerged from behind a cloud so I could see the apparition.

"You." It was the boy from the rocks. I almost laughed out loud at my silliness for expecting a spirit.

The boy said nothing, just gazed up at me through long lashes. His eyes grew wide, and he reached out a shaky hand. It appeared almost translucent—perhaps a trick of the moonlight, but once again, I felt afraid. I froze, suddenly unsure if the boy before me was in fact real or imaginary.

His lips moved as if to speak, and then he turned and sprinted for the river.

"Wait," I called after him as once more I watched the boy take a flying leap and plunge over the rocks and into the water.

He vanished, replaced by the roar of the river. Shaking, I sank to my knees.

And the world went silent.

PART III

造 反 有 理

To Rebel Is Justified

SPRING, 1969

CHAPTER 11

MING

The villagers were gathered at the work hall, whispering behind their hands instead of setting off for the fields. I was on alert, but I couldn't be sure if their murmurs were about me.

Li's bed had looked untouched that morning. He hadn't come back the night before. I scanned the crowds now, looking for his face. But he wasn't there.

I spotted Tian, and he waved me over, keeping his voice low. "Did you hear? They found a body in the river."

My heart ricocheted. Li? But before I could ask, Tian shook his head. "It was the boy from the other day. The one you and Li saved."

The boy from the ocean. He must have tried swimming again. I swallowed, unsure of what it all meant and wishing Li were here. "What happened?"

"The body got lodged on some rocks right before the river emptied into the sea. It's in Long-chi right now; they're going to take it out to sea and feed him to the fish." Tian narrowed his eyes. "You knew what he was doing, didn't you? How did he know to follow the river?"

My face flushed. Was Tian accusing me? "I—I—" But I had no words.

Tian shook his head. "Idiot," he muttered, and I wasn't sure if he was talking about the boy or me. I could hear the whispers getting louder, could feel the eyes of some of the villagers on me. I tried to ignore them, but it felt like tight walls were forming around me. The air was stifling, and it was difficult to breathe. I scanned the crowd again for a sign of Li. His absence was a knot in the pit of my stomach.

Commander Hongbing burst into the hall.

"Where is Comrade Li?" he demanded. "He hasn't reported in since last evening."

I needed to get out of there. "I'll go find him," I volunteered.

The commander grumbled, but he gave me permission to go.

I felt better once I was outside. I didn't have a clue where to look for Li, but I set off down the main road, desperate to put some distance between myself and the village. Without thinking about it, I headed into Long-chi.

My thoughts turned back to the boy. Where was he headed? Was he following the same route Ba had planned? My father's voice came rushing back to me now, a tidal wave of memory I had unknowingly kept at bay.

Following the river is just the beginning of the journey. If you were to really go to Hong Kong, you would have to cross the river at the main bend and scamper over the old rope bridge to the base of the peninsula's tallest peak. Would the bridge still be there? *From there, there is no footpath to get to the other side, but the rocks are smooth, and it wouldn't be hard to forge a path to the sea. On the other side, there would be guards and dogs, but if you managed to avoid them in the dead of the night, you could reach the beach . . .*

I snapped back to the present. The road veered left into town and right to the river. I squinted at the path to the right. Was that a break I could see in the weeds? I almost went closer to have a look, but my feet kept to the well-trod route, and while my mind considered the alternative, my body turned toward Long-chi.

The little town was busy, and there were crowds of people gathered in the square. I was relieved that nobody seemed to notice me, and I slipped past them, still keeping an eye out for Li.

I spotted him under the statue of Old Lao. He was folded up, half sitting, half squatting, his head between his knees.

"Li!"

He turned toward my voice, but it was as if he was looking right through me. His gaze was distant and unsettling, so unlike him.

His clothes were filthy, and one sleeve was torn. His hair was wild, and his eyes were sunken and dark. I was certain he hadn't slept.

"Li." My voice was soft. "Where were you? What happened last night?"

"I saw him, Ming. I saw him again. By the river." His eyes finally met mine.

The hair on the back of my neck prickled at the mention of the river. A lump rose in my throat.

"Come on, let's get you home so you can lie down a bit," I suggested. "I can tell Hongbing you're unwell—"

Li grabbed my arm so hard I could feel the individual bones of his fingers. "I saw him again, Ming. The boy. I don't know where he's from, but he came *here*. To swim. He told me so when we pulled him out of the ocean. But last night, he jumped into the river." His fingers dug even deeper, and his voice dropped to a whisper. "Was he a freedom swimmer like your father?"

But before I could answer, the crowd shifted around us. "Make way, make way." A procession was snaking through the square. Four men were carrying a makeshift stretcher slung between bamboo poles. There was a body in it, and I recognized the boy we had rescued. It was hunched over with its ear pressed to the stretcher, the clothes hanging off it in shreds. The eyes were wide open, as was the mouth, froth coating the bluish lips as if in mid-scream. As the men marched past, I recognized the look of terror in those dead eyes.

I looked away. The sight conjured up images of other bodies that had been brought through the village. I was suddenly grateful Ma hadn't let me see my father's body. I shuddered and shook my head to clear the thoughts.

Li was still gripping my arm. "That was him. That's what happened to him." His face was ashen, like he'd seen a ghost, and I was afraid he would throw up on the spot. Finally, he let go of me and sank to the ground, overcome by weariness and exhaustion.

My heart broke for him, but I couldn't find the words to say so. "Come on, Hongbing's looking for you," I said gently.

Eventually, he staggered to his feet, gripping my hand for support. I was shocked by how shattered he looked, like he had aged ten years in a single night.

We were silent on the trek back. I was hoping Li wouldn't say anything when we passed the path to the river, but to no avail.

"Why don't the villagers go to the river?" His voice was hoarse and scratchy, like it had been used for screaming. What had happened to him last night?

"Bodies. That's where we put the bodies when everyone died," I said.

"Your mother?"

I nodded.

Li pursed his lips. "Where was he going? How would he reach Hong Kong?"

My eyes were stinging, and I shut them tight, willing Li to let it go. I felt the rush of fear and panic, too used to the taunts and accusations of the villagers, and every nerve in my body wanted to run away.

But this wasn't Caocao, or the Cadre, or an official who was out to get me into trouble. This wasn't even Tian, bossing me to do something for what he insisted was my own good.

This was Li. And Li was my friend.

"My father said the easiest way to reach the other side of the peninsula was to follow the river to its biggest bend." I closed my eyes, picturing the trail for the second time today. We were utterly alone on the road, but my skin still prickled as if it could feel eyes in the weeds.

"You have to climb up the peak and back down. It's maybe four *li* to the shore. Then another four or six *li* swimming, maybe more. There are sharks and guards, but if you make it past them, there's an island—you can see it from the other side of the peninsula. I think its name means Level Land. It's not Hong Kong, but if you make it to the shore, they'll take you in to get papers—that's what the rumors are, anyway." I swallowed hard, not trusting my own thoughts. "I've never known anyone . . . not since my father . . ." Wherever my mind was going with that idea, it stopped, and my words trailed off.

Li's eyelids were heavy, and I noticed a small vein throbbing in his forehead. He didn't look up at me.

"Have you ever thought about it?"

I wasn't sure the question was meant for me, but I answered anyway, as truthfully as I could.

"Sometimes." It was more than I had admitted to anyone except Tian. "When I'm out in the fields and the sun is burning, and my arms feel like they're falling off, and I know there won't be anything but a handful of millet gruel for dinner. When the Cadre deducts our points and rations for no reason. But it's all just dreaming," I added quickly. "Like wishing you could fly."

Li nodded wearily and said no more. We walked the rest of the way in companionable silence.

When we returned to the village, Commander Hongbing was waiting for us. "What are you layabouts doing?" he barked sternly. I snapped to attention.

Hongbing stormed over to Li, practically shouting in his ear. I took a step back. "Are you a lazy fool living on the Party's hard work? Get to the fields, comrade!"

I was stunned. This was completely different from how I'd seen Hongbing act with Li in the past. These two were no longer comrades.

I opened my mouth to protest, but without another word, Li staggered toward the hall to collect his tools.

I didn't know what to do, so I followed.

★ ★ ★

We made it through a long day in the fields, squatting in the dirt, planting young peanuts in the troughs we'd dug. We were more sluggish than usual, still shaken up from the morning's events. People whispered, huddled in their family groups, and once again, I felt the glances thrown my way. I did my best to ignore them, but I was fighting back tears all day.

Li and some of the other city boys had been assigned to a new field close to mine. They looked particularly battered as they struggled up and down their rows. I kept an eye on Li. He was usually one of the hardest working of the group, but he kept stopping to lean on his tools, eyes squeezed shut and brow matted with sweat.

At the end of the day, there was a mad dash to report our day's work, as all the boys wanted to beat the queue. But Commander Hongbing made Li put in extra hours to make up for the time he'd lost in the morning. I stayed behind to watch him work by himself long after the sun had set and he was forced to work by the dim moonlight. He was a lone figure in the darkness, bent double like an animal, huffing and puffing and screaming at the earth. Finally, he set down his tools and curled up in the fetal position beside them.

I didn't need to hear his sobs to know that he was crying.

★ ★ ★

It was completely dark by the time I found him on the beach, staring out to sea. I wasn't sure if he had seen me watching him or if he would be embarrassed that I had seen him cry.

"I'm sorry about Hongbing," I finally said. "He seems worse than the Cadre."

Li sighed heavily and sprawled on his back to stare up at the stars. "It's not that, Ming. What happens when everything you ever believed in is turned on its head?" he asked, though I didn't think he expected an answer. "Like finding out that what you thought was the sun rising in the morning was actually the moon. That when you laughed, your soul was really crying. That your family is your enemy, and that you know your enemies better than your friends."

We sat in silence, Li clearly trying to work out whatever it was that had shaken him so badly.

That night, Li lay in bed, his face turned away from me. The awful day was finally over. I had no more thoughts or words of my own, so I crawled over to my bunk and pulled out my book of Mao.

★ ★ ★

The next day, Li had developed a fever. His skin was white and clammy, his whole body shaking under the covers. He could barely open his eyes, let alone stand, so Tian and I had to half carry, half drag him to the doctor's house. He stayed there all day and through the night.

On Sunday, I tucked my book of Mao quotes under my arm and set off to pick up Li for our lesson with Fei and Shu. But Nurse Xi wouldn't even let me in to see him.

"His fever won't break, and he's been delirious all night." There was no hiding the concern in her face. "I've kept a cold compress on his head so he won't burn his brain."

"Will he be okay?" I gripped the book in my hand so tightly my skin pressed into the embossed lettering.

She sighed and shook her head. "Only time will tell. But he needs to rest. Come back tomorrow, and maybe he'll be better."

Nurse Xi shut the door.

I swallowed hard and stared down at the red book in my hand. There were no answers there. I squeezed my eyes shut and remembered the prayers Ma had taught me. The shrines we used to keep in our homes had been dismantled, and we weren't supposed to worship the old deities anymore. But now, I fell to my knees and bowed my forehead to the ground three times, silently begging the gods to look after my friend.

★ ★ ★

Fei's eyes were wide as moons when she answered the door. She poked her head out, scanning left and right. "Where's Li?"

I rubbed the back of my neck, feeling the heat rise to my face. "He—uh—he's unwell."

"Oh." She seemed uncertain, like she wanted to say more.

"I—ah—guess we should cancel the lesson, then?" I stammered.

Her face fell. "Well, I mean, you know, you came all this way." She stared down at her feet. "And my aunt's not even here—she's away visiting relatives. The boys are with me, of course," she added when she realized what she'd said. I watched her face flush pink. "I mean, they're playing now, but they'll be back. I'm looking after them until she gets back tomorrow."

"Of course, of course." I nodded, and she smiled.

I mustered the courage to say, "Shall we continue with our lessons, then?"

I took the seat usually reserved for Aunt Shu, and Fei grabbed an upturned bucket and settled down beside me. She was so close I could smell her, that salty-sweet sourness that was so delectably Fei. My pulse was racing, and I felt my stomach turn over. I tried to keep my hands steady as I cracked open the book to the marked section where we had left off.

"*All reactionaries are paper tigers.*" Fei tilted her head to read over my shoulder, and I noticed the snowy whiteness of her neck. "*In appearance, reactionaries are terrifying, but in reality, they are not so powerful.*"

"Hmm," Fei mused. "Chairman Mao's a very observant man, isn't he?"

I was captivated by the lilt in her voice and just wanted her to keep talking. "How do you mean?"

"I don't think he's even talking about the Party in this case. Sure, he means the reactionaries, but isn't this true in real life too? That the things that scare us the most only frighten us because of how we perceive them? You know, like all the silly things we believe. Like that demons have possessed a baby if it cries and it's not hungry, or that the river is haunted. Who says those things are so bad, anyway? Maybe it's just in our heads."

I nodded along, drunk on her nearness. She caught me staring and shyly lowered her gaze, but I could see a small smile playing on her lips. "Sorry, I got carried away." She shifted in her seat so that our knees were almost touching. "Auntie Shu says I'm a silly girl."

"No, no, not at all. I think what you said makes perfect sense. And you're right, Chairman Mao's a smart man." I wanted to change the topic; I had no interest in the lesson at all. "Do you . . . do you still think about your sister?" I ventured.

She nodded. "I always want to go down to the river to look for her. Even though it's been so many years, it haunts my soul. Like a part of me feels that if I keep looking, she will pop out from behind a tree and say, 'Here I am!' and come back to me." She sighed and gave a little shrug. "But I'm afraid to. Because every time I don't find her, I'm a little bit more sure she's really gone."

She turned her cheek to me. Her wide eyes were framed by thin lashes. There was a stray one just on the tip of her nose. Before I knew what was happening, I reached out and caught it on my finger.

She smiled and gazed at my face. "Your eye is twitching."

"Really?" I went to cover it, but she reached out and touched my cheek, just beneath my eye.

"A twitch in your left eye means good things will come." She smiled again, and I felt my heart fluttering, my face on fire where her soft fingertips brushed my skin.

At that moment, we heard whooping and hollering accompanied by the usual stampede as the boys raced into the room. The lesson was officially over.

"Fei! Fei!" One of the boys crashed into her, nearly bowling her over with his small body. She laughed and ruffled his hair. He gave me a suspicious glare. "What's *he* doing here?"

"Kai, don't be rude," Fei scolded gently. "Ming is our teacher, but he's also our friend, so he's welcome. Now, go clean up." She dismissed her cousin with a playful punch.

"I—I should get along," I mumbled. As I stood up to go, Fei reached out and caught me by the arm.

"Would you like to stay for dinner?" She smiled playfully. "I don't think my cooking would beat my aunt's, but it'd be a change from eating with the boys."

I was grinning so much that I was sure my mouth would split in two.

CHAPTER 12

LI

Hot. Burning. My insides on fire. I wrapped myself tighter, trying to smother the blaze that scorched my lungs by curling up around it to snuff it out. But while my chest, stomach, and organs burned, my limbs trembled with cold. Fire and ice. My tortured cocoon.

Voices. Shadows. Strings of light. Some real, others visions in my head. A ghost boy. My father. Noose. On his knees. Cackling. The boy diving. Once. Twice. Leaping off the rocks. Voices again. Scolding. Shouting. More cackling. Soothing murmurs. A matron's coo.

All of it a mess in my head.

I slept and woke. I woke to be dunked in tepid well water. I slept once I was dried and wrapped up like a rice roll, steaming from the inside out. The fire inside me would not be quenched. And still I burned.

★ ★ ★

It was day four when my fever finally broke. I knew this only because the doctor's wife kept a calendar hanging over the makeshift bed. She marked off each day with a bold red pen as it passed.

I realized with a start that it was only four weeks until the New Year. I had been in the village for more than half a year.

"We're awake today." Nurse Xi smiled warmly.

I tried to smile, but it took a lot of effort. My whole body felt like it had been dragged through thick mud.

Nurse Xi came over and pressed the back of her hand against my forehead.

"The fever has definitely broken, but you're still warm. Are you hungry?"

My stomach gurgled in response, and I managed a weak laugh. "I'm sure your home cooking would set me right up."

She left to get the stove going. I leaned back against the hard pillow, sighing. I'd slept for days, but my mother's letter was still fresh in my mind. It was a dull ache, ever present though I tried to push it aside for at least a while.

Nurse Xi returned with a piping-hot bowl of plain congee that she had sprinkled with spring onions, fried garlic, and some soy sauce. Its smooth saltiness felt good, and I polished off the bowl in a few mouthfuls. The warmth spread through my muscles.

"I didn't realize you were telling the truth about my cooking," Nurse Xi said. I handed back my bowl.

"You'll spend one more night here, just to be sure, and we'll have you back to work tomorrow," she said briskly. "Rest, now. Your friend will be relieved to hear that you're up. He's been stopping by every day."

Her mention of Ming lifted my spirits even more, and I settled back down to sleep.

★ ★ ★

Ming arrived at midday. His look of relief matched Nurse Xi's, and I wondered how bad I'd been. I gave him a small wave.

"How are things?" I patted a spot on the bed, and Ming perched on the edge. "Has Feng taken over the brigade and named himself commander?"

"Not yet." Ming smiled. "We've all been worried about you. I'm glad you're okay."

"You can't get rid of me that easily," I said, and he chortled. I liked how easy it was to make him smile. "I'm looking forward to getting out of here and going back to our swimming lessons." Over the past few weeks, we'd both noticed that I could almost keep up with Ming's sure strokes.

Ming suddenly grew serious. "They're patrolling the beaches now. They won't let people in the water, not even on this side of the peninsula. No more swimming."

"Because of the boy?" I asked.

Ming dropped his gaze. "He wasn't from around here. He was from Huizhou, but he was sent to a village maybe forty *li* away for reactionary crimes. He was found with a book in English and accused of studying to be a Russian spy. He ran away and got as far as Longgang by train, then walked the rest of the way here, hiding from the guards. They found forged papers in his pockets, residency permits for different sections, including one for here.

"The water was too cold and the currents too strong. I don't think he made it much farther than that break of waves just off the rocks. Maybe he thought he could swim all the way around, or he didn't realize he was on the wrong shore." Ming shook his head. "What a stupid idea. If they'd found him alive, they'd have punished him more. He'd never have seen his family again."

The image of the boy on the rocks sprang to mind—the peaceful but determined look on his face before he plunged into the sea. *Stupid?* I was leaning more toward courageous, even if a bit foolhardy. I realized I admired him much more than the heroes in stories who fought for the glory of the Party. There was a spark in my mind that I couldn't dismiss.

"Hey, how'd the lesson go with Fei?" I remembered suddenly. "Did the demon lady spit fire at you?"

Ming flushed, his quiet shyness always there on the surface. He shuffled about and said, "Well, Aunt Shu wasn't there."

My eyebrows shot so high I thought they would crash through the worn-out tiles in Doctor Xi's roof. "She wasn't there? So, what happened?"

Ming swayed, his lips twitching.

"Fei and I had the lesson," he said finally. "And I stayed for dinner."

"Ha!" My guffaw was raucous. "Wow! Dinner? She cooked *dinner*? For just the two of you?" I knew exactly what this gesture meant.

"Her cousins were there," Ming added quickly. "It wasn't just us. But yeah, it was . . . nice."

He went on to describe the whole meal in perfect detail, praising Fei's cooking while I nodded along. I didn't particularly want to hear his ramblings about the way she spooned rice into his bowl or the artistry in how she set out chopsticks. But when it came to Fei, Ming never seemed to find it hard to say exactly what was on his mind. I listened patiently to his love-struck story.

I was happy for my friend, really happy for him—and that managed to cut through the pain of my own problems.

★ ★ ★

I slept fitfully. After days of semiconsciousness, my mind was suddenly wide-awake in the dead of night. What my family was facing came back to me in full force.

We were branded now—the family of a counterrevolutionary.

How could this be?

I refused to think about my father, but the questions wouldn't stop coming. Was he just a traitor with an easy smile? He was prone to idealist thinking; had the signs always been there?

It had to be a mistake. He had mentioned he had been awarded a government contract. Was evidence planted on him? Did someone make a false accusation? A friend or a colleague? Or was I just blind to his faults, and he really was a political criminal?

I needed answers. But Mother had said only that he'd been sent away. She didn't even know where.

My mind swam through murky thoughts.

★ ★ ★

The next morning, I went back to the dormitory. The room was empty; everyone must have already reported to the fields. I was looking for my clean shirt when I spotted a note left on my bed.

> Mister Li,
>
> Please report immediately.
>
> Commander Hongbing

I eyed it warily, noting the way he'd addressed me. *Mister*—not *comrade*. Something was amiss. I thought of my mother's letter, how it had looked tampered with. Was there anything incriminating in there?

I changed quickly and headed out. I spotted Hongbing just up the pathway in his full Red Guard uniform, arms crossed defiantly. Feng was with him.

"*Mister* Li, I am pleased to see you are back in full health," Feng said sweetly, though I detected the hint of a sneer.

I stiffened. Feng and I hadn't spoken much except about ordinary matters since the incident with Zhu. His peculiar manner put me on edge.

"Well, this village has excellent facilities. The local doctor and his wife rival the best care in the city." I pulled myself up to my full height so he would have to tilt his head to look up at me.

Hongbing broke in. "Our superiors will be pleased to hear this, as it goes to show the true value of our education program and why we are here." Feng licked his lips, almost greedily. This was serious, like the times my classmates had been forced into confession and self-criticism sessions. I was in deep trouble.

"You wanted to see me, Commander?" I asked.

"Ah, yes, Comrade Li." Hongbing had his usual confidence and air of authority, but I could tell he was a bit uncomfortable.

"Some of the team members and I—well, we would like to ask you a few questions of an official nature." He fiddled with the sleeves of his uniform. "Given that there is no official Party headquarters for our brigade in the village yet, the Cadre has kindly volunteered his own offices for us to conduct a formal interview."

"Right—right now?" I stammered. Formal interviews were for people suspected of reactionary behavior or political crimes. Depending on the accused, it could just be questions, or the Party might present "proof" to catch out liars and force confessions. The letter my mother had sent must have raised questions. My father's supposed crimes were already having an effect on my reputation, even here.

Hongbing nodded, and Feng smirked in triumph. I recognized that smugness, the accusatory gleam of the Red Guards. We'd all had the same look of righteous outrage back in school when the Cultural Revolution had first taken hold, particularly during the struggle sessions.

Master Wu was a classical music teacher who had once been a proud instructor on Russian opera and composers. When the Revolution started, he was reduced to teaching nothing more than songs praising Mao.

One day, I arrived at school to find a big-character poster draped over the main balcony. WU IS A WRETCHED WESTERN SYMPATHIZER AND RUSSIAN SPY. One of my classmates told me that someone had found Russian sheet music in Wu's collection and reported it to the leader of our local Red Guards. The headmaster and the rest of the faculty were powerless to stop us.

Wu was brought into the courtyard, the Red Guards shoving and spitting at him. They gave him a bamboo pole, weighted down on both ends with heavy buckets of stones, to carry on his shoulders. He hunched in the middle of the crowd, a dunce cap on his head, as they berated him for hours, hurling obscenities and demanding he confess to increasingly ridiculous crimes:

I am a pig Westerner who eats his own feces.

I am a pig Westerner who eats his own feces and smells his own stinky farts.

I am a pig Westerner who eats his own feces and smells his own stinky farts listening to the counterrevolutionary music of my wretched pig Westerner employers.

And on it went.

I wasn't an official member of the Red Guards then. My application had only just been submitted, and I was still waiting for the official review. But I joined in the jibes. I remembered Master Wu once boasting about being in the national orchestra and traveling overseas to play. "Maybe he was a spy," I reasoned. But, more importantly, I remembered that he had once marked down our entire class because one student had stolen a recorder from the classroom after school hours. Rather than making the culprit confess, Wu had punished the entire class. Maybe I thought he deserved the berating he was getting at the hands of the Red Guards.

Now I wasn't so sure.

Hongbing spun on his heel. Feng gestured for me to pass so that he could bring up the rear, our own little procession through the village. I was trapped like a steer on parade to the butcher.

They marched me to the work hall and threw open the door. The main room where we registered every morning was empty. Hongbing led me to the back of the hall. This was where the

Cadre and his two officials kept rooms for administrative purposes, although they rarely used them.

Hongbing opened the door and led me through to the Cadre's office.

It was a cramped room, full of dust. I guessed the Cadre had more important matters to attend to (like napping in his own home) than bothering with office upkeep. A single light bulb dangled from the ceiling, flickering due to the ancient generator that powered the building.

Hongbing motioned for me to take a seat, and Feng went to stand beside the Cadre's chair. I sat on the hard wooden stool on the opposite side of the desk while Hongbing settled into the cushioned seat of the village's top official.

He cleared his throat before beginning.

"Comrade Li, we have called you here to ask you some questions. As we all know, asking questions of ourselves and examining our motives and intentions are the revered ways to arrive at the truth, to further our commitment to the Party."

Hongbing's anxious voice told me he had never conducted a formal interview like this before.

Feng, on the other hand, was exceptionally confident. "And if we find that you are guilty, you will confess to your crimes." He was practically shouting, and I half expected him to slam his fist on the table.

"But of course we do not suspect that is the case, do we,

Comrade Feng?" Hongbing was doing his best to keep the peace.

"As we know, the practice of self-criticism is fundamental to the ideology and methodology of the Party," Hongbing went on. "As such, it is essential that we all undergo self-critiquing sessions to better understand how we may further the Party's objectives."

I rubbed my hands on my thighs and cleared my throat, dreading what was coming next.

"As such, Comrade Li"—Hongbing was repeating himself, hiding behind Party vernacular—"we invite you to please proceed with your own self-analysis and confession. A cleansing, if you will, of your political mind."

My political mind? Maybe this wasn't about my father, but I was still wary. Most Party members had gone through at least one self-criticism session, but I'd managed to avoid them so far.

I scrabbled for the right words.

"Well," I began slowly, doing my best to deepen my voice and seem more serious, "I didn't meet my commitment to educate the people and further our Party's ideology this week. I missed a lesson with my appointed village family and shirked my responsibilities in the field." This was, of course, because I had been delirious with fever, but it was a start.

Feng narrowed his eyes, clearly finding my half-hearted attempt unsatisfactory. But Hongbing nodded. "Go on."

I wondered if they were looking for a specific confession after all. "I haven't . . . reflected enough on my shortcomings to the Party. I have taken my commitment to its cause for granted and could do more to be self-aware and diligent in my own self-reproach." I smiled inwardly, but maybe I'd gone too far by confessing to not being good at confessing.

Feng was livid. "That type of smugness is exactly the sort that will not be tolerated. Your despicable bourgeois thinking needs to be eradicated from our ranks."

Hongbing held up a hand for silence. "Now, now, settle down, Comrade Feng. I'm sure that Li is trying his best." He leaned forward, and the chair let out a rude squeak. Hongbing shut his eyes momentarily to regain his composure.

"Comrade, is there anything else you would like to point to? Perhaps from a while back? It's time for us to revisit past misgivings and fully exonerate ourselves of our wrongdoings."

A while back. They were probing me, giving me a chance to come clean about something. I thought back over the past few weeks, trying to think of an incriminating act that could have brought this on.

I knew they were waiting for me to say something, so I blurted out the first thing that came to me.

"I wrote a poem. A political poem, but not about the Party." I winced, knowing that I was putting Ming under potential scrutiny. Even though I was confessing to being the author of the poem, I shouldn't have even admitted it existed.

They exchanged a look. This time, it was Feng who urged me on. "Tell us more."

I said carefully, "It was about a place, but the way it was written, now that I consider it, it may—unconsciously—have had intonations that did not reflect my true commitment to the Party."

"And why did this occur?" Feng demanded, rapping the desk with his knuckles.

I took a deep breath. "I was on the beach, thinking about something my father once told me. I had never been to the beach before, never seen the ocean. And I was inspired by my father's words." I bowed my head, trying to summon an expression of deep sorrow. "I know now that perhaps I was influenced by wayward thinking. My . . . my father was imprisoned last week."

I was weaving together the most intricate web of lies and truth.

Feng crossed his arms again, his face unreadable. Hongbing, on the other hand, looked relieved.

"Comrade, your words and frankness are refreshing," Hongbing said. "While we don't condone these actions, of course, there is little doubt of your true commitment and Communist spirit."

I stared, wide-eyed, and he turned to Feng.

"See, Comrade Feng? I knew there was nothing to worry about. A good comrade who is true of spirit and of pure thought can immediately identify moments of indiscretion and weakness. That poem you found was clearly a lapse."

So it was the poem! While Ming had decided to send Fei the letter we had worked on together, I had been so moved by its sincerity that I had asked him to copy the poem down for me as a gift. *How foolish of me!* I shuddered as I remembered taking it from Ming after he had finished writing it out. How had Feng gotten his hands on it?

Was there something more they were keeping from me? Was there still a trap? But Hongbing was smiling and nodding, and Feng seemed put out, so maybe I was in the clear.

My confidence came back to me. "Well, comrades, thank you for this humbling moment. You are right—the chance to self-criticize helps cleanse us of corruption and move toward a unified and clear objective. Commander Hongbing, I would like the opportunity to pen a self-confessional essay rehashing this session so that I might feel formally purged of my actions and reflect even further."

Now I was being smug, essentially begging for more punishment to prove just how loyal I was, but I was willing to bet a month's rations that this was the right move.

Hongbing nodded eagerly. "Of course, yes. That would be most appropriate for a true comrade. Your commitment to bettering yourself as a Party member will be noted."

Feng remained silent, but I could read the seething rage in his eyes. I tried to appear modest and meek.

My heart was racing, and my feet were a little unsteady as I staggered out of the building. I was late for work, and my day's points would reflect this, but I didn't really care. I knew I had avoided disaster, but I had a hunch that this would not be the last time.

★ ★ ★

I made it through the day, though by noon I felt ready to collapse. My muscles screamed; the fever had worn out my body. When the bell rang for the end of work, I could hardly stand long enough to report in. I couldn't be bothered thinking about dinner. I just needed to rest.

But back in the dorm, my belongings were strewn about the room, my bedding trashed. On the bunk where I slept, a long strip of paper was laid out, the message scrawled big and bold.

LI PINGZHOU IS A REACTIONARY SWINE

I snatched at the sign, tearing it into ten thousand pieces. I stormed through the room, gathering my things. The only thing untouched, of course, was *Quotations from Chairman Mao Zedong*, carefully placed on the bed.

The handwriting was generic, but it didn't really matter. I knew it was a warning—from Feng, from Hongbing, from the Party as a whole. Even though I had "passed" the interview, I was marked. My friends no longer trusted me.

I was on my own.

十 三

CHAPTER 13

MING

L i stopped coming to the lessons in the village, saying he'd convinced the commander that his Party obligations were better served elsewhere, so I instructed Fei and Aunt Shu on my own. Aunt Shu seemed to begrudgingly accept me, and Fei made an effort to hide our affection for each other in her aunt's presence.

The beginning of spring was unseasonably hot, reminding me of monsoonal late summer. My clothes clung to my skin, heavy and suffocating. The hot wind brought no relief during the days, the ground sizzling beneath our feet. Out in the fields, we baked under the sun, and I imagined we would all start popping and bubbling around the edges like fried eggs. The humid nights were unbearable, and there was little sleep for anyone.

Usually, the most exciting part of spring was the New Year. It was the most important holiday of the year, the only national holiday where we had more than a single day's rest. The whole village came together to celebrate for two weeks, and we didn't have to work for three days. While the Mid-Autumn Festival featured a few lanterns and musicians, New Year was an all-out affair with markets, fireworks, and traveling performance troupes. Colorful parades of lions and dragons could be found marching through the towns and villages, attracting festive crowds.

Usually.

Last year, the Cadre had declared that festivities across the country were officially canceled by Party decree. Villagers were expected to observe the holiday with decorum, reflecting on Communist ideals and their service to the Party. Everyone had grumbled and complained behind closed doors, but there was nothing to be done. Fortunately, we still didn't have to go to the fields, even if the festivities were no more.

This year, New Year celebrations were still canceled, but many of the villagers were even less interested in three days of solemn reflection and made arrangements to visit family in other villages or even the city. The city boys were eager to finally make the trip home and see their families for the first time since they had arrived almost eight months ago.

All except Li.

Li had become more withdrawn. Feng and the others had started treating him differently, and he'd become an outcast, keeping to himself.

The week before the New Year, Fei pulled me aside after our lesson, out of earshot of her aunt. "Aunt Shu is going to visit her cousin in another village. I have to look after the boys on my own." She dropped her eyes to her feet. "I thought maybe you could give us some extra lessons?"

★ ★ ★

Finally, it was the New Year, and hardly anyone was left in the village. Tian had even organized for a few of the older boys to go into Tanshui, a small city, which meant an hour's walk to the closest bus stop and another two hours on a crowded, hot bus.

"Little Brother." Tian's greeting was gruff, his voice deeper than ever. He was eighteen now. He'd moved out of the bunks and been transferred to one of the adult work units, so I hardly saw him anymore.

"Hi." I held his gaze. I was different too.

"How's things?"

I shrugged. "Good, you know."

"We're headed into Tanshui for a 'revolutionary field trip.'" Calling it a revolutionary field trip was how he had convinced the Cadre to let him leave the village without any family to visit. "You should come with us. See some new sights, new people; it'll do you some good to visit a proper city. Get out of this place. Wang and Cho are coming." He nodded to his former dorm mates a short distance away.

"That's okay. Maybe next time." I gave him another smile, a

big one, to let him know I was okay. Tian had always looked after me. But I didn't need looking after anymore. And I knew why.

Fei.

"All right." He clapped me on the shoulder and gave it a squeeze.

I caught Li after breakfast. I thought this would be the perfect time to fit in some swimming lessons. He had greatly improved; his athletic body was built for endurance, so he was practically keeping up with me. We'd had to stop our lessons when guards had started patrolling the beaches, but I had a new idea.

He jumped when I grabbed his arm, and I noticed how skinny he'd become. The lean body hardened by field work was rail thin.

"Ming." His face softened when he saw it was me. His eyes were dark and haunted, his cheeks hollow.

"You look like you haven't slept in days," I said.

Li shook his head. Maybe it was my imagination, but he seemed to be fighting back tears. "It's a tiresome journey, my friend."

"What's wrong?"

Li sighed again. "The village is different now. There are eyes and ears everywhere."

I gnawed on my lip. He was sounding more like crazy old Zhu than my friend. I needed to cheer him up and take his mind off things. "I'm meeting Fei and her cousins for a swim. You should come."

Li shook his head, but I took him by the arm anyway. He didn't put up a struggle and allowed me to pull him along.

Fei was waiting for us at a crossroads between our villages, her cousins screaming and laughing. She waved to me, and my spirits lifted. "Ming! Li!" My name was a melodious note coming from her lips.

I waved back, my eyes on her as she came toward us.

Li's scowl dissolved. "It's been too long, Miss Fei. You have grown more elegant and beautiful since we last met." He gave a courtly bow.

I shoved aside a pang of jealousy, especially when Fei let out a giggle and returned his bow with an awkward one of her own. I still had so much to learn.

"Hey, Kai." I playfully punched the oldest cousin in the arm. We'd become friends since that first dinner we had shared, bonding over kung fu stories. He gave me his best praying mantis stance before launching into a series of air chops and half kicks that made him look like he was fighting off a gang of mosquitoes.

Fei tsked and wagged her finger. "Kai, don't be such a ruffian. Set a good example for your brothers. And you shouldn't be encouraging him," she said, turning to me.

I gave her a grin and waggled my eyebrows.

Li laughed out loud. The worry lines on his face had faded, and his eyes sparked with mischief.

The sun was climbing, and the day was already sticky and uncomfortable, but we all giggled and grinned. We walked quickly into the dense trees, seeking the cool comfort of the shade.

I was the one who had suggested going to the river for a swim. I knew Li didn't believe the river was haunted, and Fei's cousins were too young to remember, so I only had to convince Fei. She was terrified at first, but it was the only place that we could be certain we would be alone. Even with her three small cousins and Li accompanying us, young people of the opposite sex simply didn't spend time together, and we couldn't risk the potential scandal. Finally, she had relented.

Now she was the one leading the way. I walked just behind, admiring her boldness. I'd never been to this part of the river before. We were far upstream where the water was calmer, a soothing babble rather than a deafening roar. She was sure-footed, confidently picking her way along the overgrown path.

Li followed slowly, turning this way and that, taking in every bent leaf, turned rock, and dangling twig. I wondered what he was thinking as he etched every detail of his surroundings into his mind.

I thought of Ma and how long it had been since I'd come here. But I felt oddly content as the three of us walked side by side, lost in our own worlds. Without thinking too much about what it meant, I put an arm around Fei's shoulders.

Her eyes widened, and she stared up at me. I bit my lip but didn't let go.

And then she folded up against me, small and frail, resting her cheek against my chest. I held her, and we just stood together, clasping each other in this moment.

"All right, even the city boy's getting a little uncomfortable here," Li grumbled as he went past.

We hiked on in silence. Fei led us down a steep hill, the path covered in slippery leaves. She took a graceful leap to the bottom and glanced up expectantly. I half slid and half ran down, but Li lost his footing and slid part of the way on his bottom. When he finally reached us, he was covered in mud and leaves.

"*Hai-yah!*" The cry came from all around us, and I jumped as a rapid shadow whizzed by. One of Fei's cousins was racing toward the water.

"Ru, be careful!" Fei was already scolding, but it was no use. The boy scrabbled up a wet rock and launched himself expertly, curling up into a tight ball so that he landed with a splash.

Water sprayed everywhere, spattering our faces and clothes. It felt cool and refreshing, a welcome relief. Ru bobbed to the surface, laughing maniacally, and Kai propelled himself into the water with a loud plop. The youngest of the brothers, Zhi, stayed by Fei's side, clutching at her trousers.

I let out an almighty yell, pulling my shirt over my head and tossing it to the side. My eyes fixed on that large rock, I ran for the edge and leapt.

I spread my limbs as wide as they would go, feeling the cool air as I fell. The boys scrambled away, making room as I hurtled toward the water.

The cold hit me. Flowing straight down from the mountain, the water was crisp and pure. The cool seeped into my bones.

I let myself sink. Through the murk, I could make out a few pairs of kicking feet, some bubbles, and a few minnows darting about.

Finally, my lungs screaming, I broke the surface of the water.

"Ming!" There was no mistaking the relief in Fei's voice. She and Li were leaning over the bank. I couldn't help but beam as I tossed my head back and flashed them a wicked grin.

"This is fantastic! Come on, Li!" I ducked back under, letting my hands and feet propel me forward.

Li landed with a muffled splash, and I jetted back to the surface. He was smiling, his eyes wide. He smacked the surface of the water with both palms. *"Hou ye!"* His voice cut through the silent trees, sending birds scattering from their branches.

Splash! Li whirled around to find Kai giggling and thrashing his arms about. He raised his hands like claws as the playful fighting gave way to a chase.

I turned back to the bank. Fei was perched daintily on a flat rock, her feet skimming the water, Zhi still beside her. I beckoned her over, but she shook her head. "I don't want to get wet," she said, laughing.

I shook my head, her laughter washing over me. I sank back into the river, listening to the shouts, giggles, and splashes as Li and the boys dove in and climbed back out of the water. After a while, little Zhi came in off the rock, urged on by his brothers. Only Fei stayed on the bank.

Eventually, their voices faded so that I was left with little but the rhythm of my own breath. And instead of closing my eyes and conjuring up Fei's cheerful face from memory, I could keep them open and watch her fending off the spray from her young cousins.

"Fei! Watch this," Ru called from upstream, waving his arms about. He took a deep breath and disappeared under the water. Then a pair of legs emerged from the surface, forming a wide V.

"Ru, be careful!" Fei bent forward and leaned way out so that her long braid was almost touching the water.

"Make way!" Li was once again barreling toward the bank like a typhoon. He hurled himself halfway up the rock using one arm, and with the other, he scooped up Fei, grabbing her around the waist. Before she could even cry out, she was in the water, her plait whipping around, water spraying everywhere.

Li and Ru, the coconspirators, congratulated themselves on a job well done while I watched, horrified, to see how Fei would react.

She rubbed her eyes and spat out some river water. Her threadbare top clung to her, and despite the situation, I couldn't help but notice the way it hugged her chest. It seemed like forever had passed when she finally spoke.

"I'm going to get you, you little monster!" she shrieked, and lunged for her cousin.

Ru ducked out of the way, but not before sending a torrent of water up at her. They laughed and giggled as they wrestled, Fei's earlier hesitation forgotten. Li threw himself back into the fray, grabbing Fei around the waist to throw her into the water, pretending to hold her down. She managed to break free and tried to force him under, almost climbing onto his back. The unsettled pang returned as I watched them, not knowing what to do.

"Ping zai? Is that you?"

The voice came from the other side of the river. We froze, scanning the riverbank. A guard? A villager? But the man crouching by the tree trunk was not familiar. He was caked in mud, his clothes torn, his sandals falling apart. He staggered forward, arms outstretched, and called out again.

"Ping zai! It's me. It's me!"

I backed away slowly, shielding Fei as the boys cowered behind her. *He must be crazy*, I thought, some lunatic from a nearby village. Unless he was Gong Gong the water demon, looking for prey along the river. I was regretting coming to the river; maybe it was haunted after all.

Li was staring at the man, frozen in fear.

"Father?"

十 四

CHAPTER 14

LI

Ghost. The ghost of a man was like a memory of my father. It used his voice, though it sounded crackly and hoarse rather than proud like I remembered. It called my name, the name only my parents and grandparents had ever used. The ghost had tears in its sunken eyes, wild as they bored into me.

The ghost lumbered toward me, its movements jerky as it toppled into the river, still calling me by my nickname. "Ping zai! Ping zai, it's really you!"

Even with the river between us, there was no masking the stench. (Ghosts didn't smell, did they?) I was rooted to the spot, my muscles beyond my control, as the ghost that resembled my father came up to me and reached out its skinny arms.

"Ping zai! It's me. It's Father."

My eyes stung and blurred, but I still didn't move. I just watched through the cloud of tears as he put those bony limbs around me and sobbed against my chest. "Ping zai. My dear,

dear, dear son. I found you. I found you." Dirty claws dug into my shoulders as the man wailed, his cries growing louder by the moment.

Something inside me snapped.

I shoved at the man with all my might. He sprawled in the water so that I had to climb around him.

"Son!" he cried, reaching out again. I ignored him and waded to the bank, tears running down my cheeks.

The man caught me by the ankle. "Ping zai. Don't go. Please, don't go." His voice gouged at my insides. I opened my mouth to say something, to scream or yell or cry, but no sound came out.

So I kicked his hand away and scrabbled up the bank.

"Li! Li!" I heard the distant cries but kept going.

I stumbled through the forest blindly, branches and thorns tearing my skin so little streams of blood trickled down my exposed arms, but I didn't care. I fought my way forward until I lost my footing and couldn't haul myself back up. Then I crawled, clutching at dirt and leaves. And when I was completely spent, I sank down into the mud, pressing my wet cheek against the earth.

I squeezed my eyes shut, but the images wouldn't go away, nor would the questions.

I sobbed once. Twice. And then I couldn't stop.

Ming found me like that. He pulled me up by the shoulders, cradling my head. He didn't say anything, just held me, letting me cry myself out. When I had no more energy left, he helped me rest against a tree. I couldn't look up, just stared blankly at a patch of dirt in front of me.

We stayed that way until the shadows on the forest floor began to lengthen. Finally, I lifted my head. Ming met my gaze and answered my unspoken question.

"Fei's taken him to my old house. It's abandoned. No one will find him there," he said.

I managed a nod and leaned my head back against the tree trunk, letting out a sigh. "Did he say anything?"

Ming shook his head. "Not much. Fei sent the boys home and took him to get cleaned up. Don't worry, they're sworn to secrecy. They won't tell." I was grateful to my friends; I knew the risk they were taking, harboring a fugitive.

"Thank you, my friend." We clasped hands firmly. I tried standing but slipped back against the tree. Ming helped me, and I finally staggered to my feet. I felt a hundred years old.

With my arm draped across Ming's back, the two of us slowly made our way out of the forest. As we got closer to the village, we headed toward the beach.

I had never really noticed the ramshackle hut on this part of the shore. I would have assumed it was an abandoned shed or outhouse, but of course there was no such thing in a poor village. It was a house, tiny and shoddily built. Ming led the way, his feet finding the overgrown path to his childhood home.

The door was ajar, a few bent nails sticking out of the frame, and I could hear soft voices inside. My whole body stiffened, but

Ming coaxed me along, encouraging me those last few steps. I took a deep breath and pushed open the door.

My father sat cross-legged on what would have been the old family bed while Fei sat on the lone stool. A fire was lit in the stove and some water boiled for tea. My father had washed his face and arms, so that awful smell of rot was gone.

His bones were protruding through his paper-thin skin. His face was sunken, one of his eyes was swollen completely shut, and there was a huge bruise on his left cheek.

"Father."

Fei dipped her head and stood. I hovered in the middle of the room until Ming dusted off an old wooden bucket and offered it as a seat.

I perched on the bucket opposite my father. He rocked back and forth, a chipped teacup clutched in his bony, trembling hands.

"So, are you a fugitive as well as a traitor now?"

Father winced.

"Son," he sighed. "For what it's worth, I'm sorry."

And with that weak apology, the dam inside me burst.

"Sorry? How could you? You have brought shame and ruin to the family. We have lost all respect for you." I leapt to my feet, sending the bucket clattering onto its side. "You left Mother by herself, and now nobody will even speak to her. Tze can never find a good job now—his future is ruined. Pearl has been kicked out of the Little Red Guards. We are pariahs, treated like vermin. We might as well all be dead."

Tears were blurring my vision as I stared down at him. He remained silent, peering at me pathetically. I wanted to grab him by the neck—he was so thin I could have done it with one hand—grab him and shake him until he jingled with answers.

"Why did you come here?" I spat.

"The labor camp I was assigned to is only about twenty *li* from here," he said. "I paid someone to tell them I was sick and then snuck out. I hid from the dogs and only traveled at night, following the shoreline. I came to find you straightaway, son. I . . . I wanted to explain. I need you to understand that I never meant to hurt you or your ma."

His words did nothing to curb my anger. "So tell me, then. What was your crime? Why were you taken in?"

My father closed his eyes. "An old friend who owned a tea house was imprisoned last year. He needed to deliver a letter overseas. I helped him send it."

I felt sick. *A letter overseas.* It wasn't even his. Why would he associate with such dangerous characters? Just by agreeing to help this traitor, he had doomed our family forever.

His lip trembled, and his voice cracked. "Son, you have to believe me. I have done nothing but adhere to and honor the teachings of Chairman Mao. I am not a traitor. I gave a man my word, and I honored that word. And if that makes me a reactionary and counterrevolutionary in the eyes of the so-called People's Party, then I guess that is what I must be."

I felt the sting on my palm before I realized what I'd done. My father's face was so sunken that there hadn't even been the fleshy sound of a slap, just a muted thud. He stared up at me, his hand pressed over his cheek where I had struck him.

"How can you say that?" I spat at him. "You've betrayed your country and family. You are worse than a dog. You are nothing. You are despicable."

My father didn't answer, just hung his head in shame, which only enraged me even more. I raised my hand, ready to strike him again.

Strong arms grabbed me, pulling me away. "Come on, Li. Let's go, give him some time," Ming said softly.

He gripped my shoulders and steered me away from the bed.

"I'll stay with him," he offered. "You and Fei should go home. Someone will notice if we're all missing."

I let myself calm down, though a quick glance back at the bed almost set me off again. Eventually, Fei took me by the arm and led me to the door. She pulled it shut behind us.

My voice dropped to a whisper. "They'll lock him away forever if they find him. Solitary imprisonment or worse." I didn't want to think about worse.

"It's okay. We won't let them," she said simply. I smiled, grateful that here, I didn't need to doubt my friends.

★ ★ ★

The villagers began to return as the New Year holiday came to an end. My father was still at the house, and Ming had been watching over him the past couple of days, sneaking in scraps of food from his own rations. Ming and I were still swimming, but I couldn't bear to go inside the house and face my father, though I was still worried about what to do with him. If anyone found out he was here, we would both be punished.

"Where've you been?" Feng asked as we took our meal on the last evening of the holiday.

"Just went for a swim," I said. Ever since my interrogation, Feng had developed a habit of questioning me.

"You didn't come to the city. We showed some of the villagers the inner workings of a Communist Youth League, and you missed the chance to participate. A good Party member puts the interests of the people ahead of his own."

"I'm still not feeling very well," I stammered. "I thought it best to rest up so I can continue our good work with full strength."

Feng narrowed his eyes. "We are required to help the peasants and do Chairman Mao's good work. I am sorry that you didn't *feel* you were up to the task. Though I can see that perhaps confronting the disgrace of your family would be too much." Feng arched an eyebrow.

I swallowed hard. Feng's mention of my family made me nervous. The sooner my father was out of my mind, the better.

★ ★ ★

That night, the dormitory was alive again with the sounds of snoring from the beds beside mine. But I couldn't sleep. Every time I shut my eyes, I saw Feng's accusing glare.

I crept out into the still night. The houses were quiet, and just one or two kerosene lamps penetrated the darkness. A stray cat hissed when I came too close to her mangy litter, but nothing else made a sound.

I stumbled when I got close to the little mud hut by the beach. My legs were shaking, and I could hear my own heartbeat in the still night.

Suddenly, shouting erupted behind me, and I spun around.

"There he is!" a voice cried out. A lamp bobbed up and down, illuminating a mob of silhouettes rushing toward me.

A wave of panic gripped me, and I fumbled up the path, reaching for the latch.

The door flew open, and my father's ghostly face stared back at me.

Hands grabbed me from both sides, and I was trapped in a tugging match between them until another hand seized the back of my collar. I screamed as I was yanked from my father's grasp and landed face-first in the dirt.

"Li Pingzhou!" I would have recognized that voice anywhere. "You have been caught harboring a reactionary criminal! You are a traitor and an enemy to the People's Party and must be suitably punished." Feng spat, and I felt the warm splat on my neck.

There was a soft thud behind me. I squeezed my eyes shut when I heard my father's plea. "Please. He's my son. Let him go. He's done nothing wrong."

"Be quiet, swine!" It was the Cadre's son, Caocao. Ming had warned me that he was a bully, and I was pretty sure I was about to see that firsthand.

I was on my knees now. "You lot are despicable." Feng grabbed me by the hair so my head snapped back. "What vile acts have you been plotting with our enemies?"

He spat on me again. My father groaned, and Caocao cackled. I counted four village boys holding my father. At least three pairs of hands held me down, but it was too dark to see anyone's face. Kamshui? Ah-Jun? Had the comrades I worked beside every day all turned on me?

"What's the meaning of all this?" The Cadre had arrived with a few of the Party officials. I tried to stand, but a sharp kick to the base of my spine sent me sprawling to the ground. A bright torch beam shone into my eyes. "Comrade Li?" The Cadre sounded confused.

"He's a sympathizer, Cadre," Feng exclaimed. "Li here has been harboring a capitalist pig, an escaped fugitive from one of the labor camps up north. The guards have been looking for him since New Year."

"They're both traitors," Caocao said.

My father groaned again before he spoke. "Please, Cadre. My son has nothing to do with this. I was the one who escaped from the labor camp. I came looking for him. He didn't know anything."

More footsteps and voices approached. The villagers had been woken up by the commotion. They carried swaying lanterns and spoke in hushed voices, amplified in the still night.

"What's going on?"

"Who is that? Is that Li?"

"Who's that man with him?"

"He looks like a vagrant."

"Reactionary swine." Caocao kicked my father and pushed his face into the ground. "We should string him up as an example."

The boys began beating him. The crowd did nothing to stop them. One or two of the villagers stepped forward and began to yell obscenities.

"Confess your crimes!" a voice called out. "Who is this foreigner-lover?"

The names and accusations were flying.

Then came a familiar cry. *"Li!"*

Ming was pushing through the crowd, trying to reach us. But at the last second, an arm pulled him away.

"Let go of me, Tian." I heard them struggling but couldn't see what was going on. I writhed against my captors, but they kept a firm grip.

"Is that your conspirator, Li? Should I bring him out here too?" Feng hissed in my ear.

"No!" I gasped, tears stinging my eyes. I expected Feng to command the crowd to bring Ming out, to make him kneel before everyone as well, but the call never came.

Instead, Feng kicked me again, and I was in the dirt. But the pain in my back was nothing next to what my father was enduring.

"You call yourself a father?" The Cadre's voice was shrill. "You dare to show your face here? Your son must be mortified. How could you bear to bring such shame to your family?"

"Please, Cadre, sir, find mercy in your heart and let him go." Despite the beating, my father's voice was suddenly strong.

The Cadre turned to me. "Denounce your father. Call him out for the pig he is."

I sobbed into the earth.

"Do it, son. I am worthless to you as a father. Denounce me and spare yourself."

"Get them up." Hands grabbed me under the armpits, and I was dragged onto my knees to face my father. The villagers pushed and shoved one another, clawing their way closer to the action.

"Denounce him!" the Cadre shouted in my face. "Denounce this capitalist pig and political enemy. He is not your father. Say it!"

My face was wet and sticky with tears and mud. I bit my lip and looked at my battered father. His head drooped to the side, and there was a gash on his cheek. The bruised eye was now swollen shut. "Do it, son. Denounce me. I am no father. The Cadre is right." Caocao struck him, and he cried out.

"This is your last chance, Li." My vision blurred, and the Cadre's voice sounded distant and cloudy. "Are you loyal to the Party or to this enemy of China? Which side are you on?"

My head throbbed, and I squinted between the men's forms.

"Denounce him."

"Put him in his place, Li!"

"Call him the swine that he is."

They were the voices of my fellow comrades, the boys I called friends, shrieking like they were possessed. In the chaos, I could have sworn Feng's face had morphed into that of a banshee with fangs.

I squeezed my eyes shut but didn't say a word, just bit my lip and choked back sobs. I'd seen other boys do this—many of my peers had written big-character posters condemning their parents for being class enemies. But despite everything, all my anger and hatred for his betrayal, he was still my father, and I could not bring myself to denounce him.

Feng spat at me once more.

They continued to beat us, taunt us. The Cadre demanded a bucket of water from the well, and our tormentors took turns dunking our heads in and holding them under.

I must have passed out at some point. The next thing I knew, I was being pulled to my feet. But the arms that held me this time were gentle. I managed to hold my eyes open long enough to see my rescuer.

"Ming." But the name came out as a splutter, my mouth too swollen and full of blood to thank him.

He carried me into the mud house and laid me out on the bed frame. There was nothing but darkness and the chirruping of crickets as I slipped into the blackness.

十五

CHAPTER 15

MING

They sent Li's father away early in the morning. Before the sun had cracked over the horizon, a truck had already been arranged for his transport back to the labor camp.

I checked on Li, who was still sleeping. He'd spent most of the night wheezing and coughing up blood. I'd had to turn him on his side so he wouldn't choke.

The next week dragged on. Out in the fields, my mouth was full of the bitter taste of sickness. I managed to keep going, knowing Fei would be waiting for me at the end of the week. I wondered if news of Li's father had reached Long-chi; it must have by now. I hoped Aunt Shu wouldn't stop our lessons.

I rushed back to the dorm and grabbed my book of Mao quotations. My forehead felt clammy, and I was shivering with the beginnings of a fever, but I refused to give in to it.

But when I got to the house, I knew something was wrong.

The laundry was still hanging outside, and Fei always brought it into the house before she sat down for a lesson. The chimney wasn't billowing with the usual plume of smoke. It was too quiet.

I rapped on the door.

It swung open immediately to a disheveled Ru. He had a fat lip, turned down and wobbling so that he looked much younger than his ten years.

"Ru, what's wrong? Where's Fei?"

"She's gone."

"What do you mean? Where would she go?" Panic took over. I didn't want to hear his response.

"Ru, who's at the door?" Shuffling footsteps approached, and the door was yanked open so hard the wooden hinges squeaked in protest.

"It's *you*." Aunt Shu's icy glare cut like slivers and needles. "You insufferable cad. You have caused nothing but trouble." She swung at me with her wooden spoon. I blocked the blow with my forearm.

She kept swiping at me, screaming, "You've ruined our family, destroyed our name! Your father was a traitor who brought shame to his family, and you have done the same to mine. You brought that prisoner's son into my house. And you dare spend time with Fei on your own? You have ruined my niece's honor so she will never find a decent husband. Your parents aren't here to beat you, so I'm going to do it for them."

I ducked out of the way as best I could. Aunt Shu was stout and strong, and though I could have overpowered her easily, filial respect kept me from striking back. Instead, I used my arms to shield myself as best as I could.

"Please, I just want to talk to Fei." I winced as the wood rapped against my bony knuckle. "Please, just let me talk to her, only for a minute, and I'll go away, I promise."

"You worthless piece of dirt. I'm going to beat you to death!" She was shrieking high enough to summon the she-demons. "You think you have a chance with her, filling her mind with garbage? Love! She said she was in love!"

My heart leapt despite the blows raining down on me. *Love? She said she was in love?* "Aunt Shu, please, can I just speak to her?"

"'Aunt Shu!' Don't you dare Aunt Shu me!" Her blows weakened, but the fury of her voice didn't diminish. "She's completely worthless for marriage now. I was lucky I could convince my cousin to take her off my hands."

I dropped my arms and was cuffed on the ear, but I hardly noticed. "What do you mean, someone took her? Where is Fei?"

Aunt Shu put her hands on her hips, a tiny smirk of triumph emerging. "She's gone. She moved to her husband's house. It's done. No wedding, no ceremony, just the bride price. And he stiffed me, the worthless clod."

"G-gone? Husband?" My mouth formed the words, but the rest of me was numb.

"She's gone for good. I told her if she dared show her face here again, I would beat her until her legs broke, and she'd have to crawl back to her husband. I won't have an idle layabout in my house." She shook her head and turned back into the house. "Love. Sik si laa!"

And she slammed the door behind her.

I sank to the ground, pressing my fists against my eye sockets to keep the tears at bay, but to no avail. It was a joke, surely. Any minute now, Fei would open the door, all smiles and laughter. Or she was just down at the well fetching water and would be surprised to find me sobbing at her door.

I heard shrieks from inside—a boy on the receiving end of one of Aunt Shu's savage beatings. I couldn't move from my spot.

If I left, if I walked away, it would mean she was really gone.

★ ★ ★

I must have fallen asleep, because the next thing I knew, someone was shaking me.

"Ming, come on. You can't stay here." It was Ru. The trembling lip was now split wide open.

I was curled up in the dirt, my hands shoved into my armpits for warmth. Slowly, I pulled myself up. I was shivering from the cold, but my insides felt like they were on fire. My neck burned my hand as I tried to massage the stiffness out of it.

"You have to go before she finds out you're still here."

"Okay." I cleared my throat. "Is she really gone?"

Ru nodded, tears spilling over his cheeks. When he rubbed at them, I saw he had something in his hand. He pressed the slip of paper into my palm and didn't say anything more.

I wanted to offer some words of comfort, but what did I have to give?

Instead, I ruffled Ru's hair and said the only thing I could think of. "Be good."

And I left him on his doorstep and slowly limped away.

★ ★ ★

On the walk back to the village, I unfolded Fei's last letter.

My dear friend Ming,

I shouldn't be writing to you—my husband, Lo, would be very angry with me if he discovered me exchanging letters with a man. I just wanted to apologize for not telling you what was happening. I wanted to, but Aunt Shu didn't even give me time to pack a bag.

I am at a village quite far from home. It is cooler, far inland, so the air is dry and the wind cuts into your skin like sharp paper. I have been quite sick since arriving but am trying to regain my strength. My mother-in-law keeps me very busy with all the things that must be done around the house. She is very strict, even more so than Aunt Shu! But sometimes she shows me kindness. She is hoping I will have a son for her soon.

I don't want you to worry about me, Ming. I miss the village very much, but I know that there is no point in holding on to the past. You showed me that. Instead, I will try to build new memories.

Take care of yourself, Ming. I hope with all my heart that you can one day be free.

May your heart be forever true,

Fei

There was no return address. I read the letter once, twice, and then crumpled up the page and flung it into the grass.

Fei was gone.

There was nothing but the sounds of frogs and crickets chirruping around me. It was late. I followed the path down toward the beach. The old house stood like a foreboding fortress in the darkness.

I pushed open the door and peered inside.

Li was sitting cross-legged on the bed beneath the mosquito netting, staring at nothing. Neither of us could face the dormitory anymore and were hiding in my house to avoid the others. It didn't matter though. Every night, Caocao and Feng rounded up the boys to drag Li outside for another struggle session. Luckily, they weren't nearly as brutal as they had been the first time, but they beat him over and over, demanding confessions for ridiculous crimes.

"I knew from the moment I met you that you were a swine and a class enemy," Feng spat, and slapped his already-bruised face.

The accusations grew wilder when Li remained largely silent except to cough and spit up blood.

"Admit it—you and your father were plotting to kill my father," Caocao cackled.

The first night, two of the boys restrained me, and I was forced to listen to my friend's cries. After that, I stayed away, completely helpless and unable to aid my friend.

The Cadre and the Party officials did not attend these beatings, but they did nothing to discourage them. I was surprised that the arrogant Commander Hongbing chose not to take part.

I knew it was only a matter of time before Li was taken away, but the order hadn't come. It was like waiting for Death to claim him.

Li lifted his head when he heard me enter. His eye was swollen and bloody from yet another beating, but in the moonlight, he was still stark and handsome. I went to a get a wet cloth to help him clean up. As I wiped the blood off his face, he gave me a small, sad smile.

"We should do the swim, Ming. You and me, we should go to Hong Kong."

十 六
CHAPTER 16
LI

My heart began to race as I waited for Ming's reply.

He looked stunned for a minute and then started laughing, loud enough for his voice to echo through the tiny room. "Good one, Li. I almost believed you. Nice joke."

I shook my head. "I'm serious, Ming. I've got it figured out." I'd spent hours going over the scenario in my mind, remembering when the trucks had first brought us into the village. *Was that really only nine months ago?* "Like your father said, if we follow the river and climb the peak at night, we have less of a chance of being spotted."

"No way. Have you forgotten the dogs? They'll sniff us out."

"We'll coat ourselves in mud, dump our clothes, throw them off the scent." I beamed at my own cleverness.

Ming shook his head. "Even *if*—and that's a big *if*—we made it to the water, there are sharks. And boat patrols. Not to mention the fact that it's a long way. Even the fittest villagers would struggle, and you've only just learned to swim."

"Come on, give yourself more credit. You're a good teacher. I'm as good as you now, and you know it." I frowned, put off by his hesitation. "I've made up my mind already. I'm not staying to be beaten every night."

He opened his mouth to protest, but the words never came. I already knew what he was thinking.

Fei was gone. I'd overheard someone from Long-chi saying she'd been sold to a Party member from another village. "She's lucky to be a good comrade's wife," Feng had said.

It was over. There was nothing left for Ming here.

And he knew it. A look of steely determination came over his face. He seemed older, angrier. I wondered if this was what his father had looked like.

A gust of wind blew through the hut, fluttering the mosquito netting. It echoed around the room like a voice laughing. I wasn't superstitious, but the sound made me shudder.

Ming heard it too, but his expression seemed even more steadfast.

"Okay," he finally said. "I'm in."

A tiny flutter of excitement twisted in my stomach, and I momentarily forgot our sorrows.

We were going to Hong Kong.

十七
CHAPTER 17
MING

The rainy season was over, but that meant typhoon season was just around the corner, so Li and I had just a few days of guaranteed calm. We needed to act fast. We spent a long night at the top of the peak, peering down at the shoreline for the telltale bobbing lights of the patrolling guards. In the distance, there was a small light, too low to be a star, too bright to be a figment of our imagination. Li guessed it was a light from the island.

"Two sweeps, which means we have to make sure they're at the farthest points when we get on the ground." Li scribbled furiously. "We should climb the peak after everyone's gone to bed and time our descent. If we get to the beach a couple of hours before dawn, we should have enough cover to reach the island. You said there are guards there?"

I nodded. "That's what my father said. They patrol and take any escapees they find to Kowloon to be registered and receive their resident IDs."

I had been a little hesitant when Li had first brought up the idea of escaping, but now I couldn't imagine doing anything else. It was what my father would have wanted—I was sure of it. Hong Kong was my legacy.

"Are you sure about that part?" Li frowned. "It seems strange that they would just take us in like that. Don't we need papers or something?"

I shook my head. "It's Hong Kong, Li. There's freedom and opportunity; it's not like China, where you have to tell the Party when you fart."

Li cracked a small smile. I was glad to be going with him. Last summer, I didn't think I would ever have the nerve to make the trip my father hadn't finished, much less with a city boy.

In the hut, after his forced nightly struggle session, Li was studying his notes, his brow creased in thought. "I don't know, Ming. Maybe we need to wait. The water's not good. You were probably right; I need more lessons." He shook his head, scrunching the pages. "We're not ready. We need more time."

I couldn't believe my ears. "Li, this was your idea. What's going on?"

There was a loud rapping on the door. We jumped in surprise and turned to each other wide-eyed, the same thought in both our minds. We'd been found out.

Another knock and an angry voice. "Li, open up." It was Hongbing.

"Coming." Li shoved the notes into his shirt and hurried to the door. The moment he opened it, Hongbing blew in. He glanced at me before turning to Li.

Hongbing reached into his pocket and pulled out a plain envelope, its seal already undone. "I'm sorry to inform you that your father is dead. He never made it back to the labor camp." The commander pressed his lips together and held out the notice. "Comrade Li, I am sorry."

Li tried to hide his pained expression. "I am . . . I am grateful that you let me know, Commander. Thank you." He took the envelope.

Commander Hongbing nodded and turned to leave. Not until his footsteps had faded did Li let the tears fall.

I rose on shaking legs, my heart pounding. I knew what had to happen. Despite this being Li's plan, it was up to me to make the final decision. And I was ready.

"Li." I was conscious of the walls and windows, suddenly terrified someone could be listening. I kept my voice at a whisper. "Li, it's time."

Li simply nodded.

★ ★ ★

We waited for the village to turn in, watching the lamps wink out one by one. But when it was time, the thick cloud cover made it almost impossible to navigate. We couldn't risk a light, so we had no choice but to stumble along in the dark.

"Will you calm down?" Li hissed when I started at a stray cat. "Do you want to tell the whole village we're leaving?"

After that, I managed to limit myself to squeezing my eyes shut and biting my lip.

We followed the river, keeping the sound of the gentle rippling to our left. It took a sharp turn to the right, which meant we would soon find the rope bridge to cross it, just as we had the night before. The bridge led us to an overgrown path that ended at the base of the peninsula's highest peak. Focused on walking, we remained silent as we began the climb. My heart was galloping, and every breath sounded deafening. Little noises in the night had me on high alert.

Eventually, we came to the top of the peak. I was surprised to find that despite the overcast sky, the view was clear, and it was easy to see out. Most importantly, we could make out the tiny light in the distance. The sea was surprisingly calm, just a few strong currents in the usual spots to avoid, nothing too difficult. These were all good omens for us.

Li pointed to two spots below where the guards would be so we could track their movements in our minds through the night, just as we had rehearsed. I could imagine their silhouettes and movements in the darkness and shuddered.

When it was time, I followed Li down the side of the mountain, my heart in my throat as my feet scrabbled to find a hold. We were moving quickly, sending rocks and gravel tumbling down below us. I imagined them raining down past the guards, alerting them to our presence.

I clenched my fists and focused on my feet, trying to keep my breathing even.

The climb down was quick, though the going was rough as there was no trail to follow. We stumbled around fallen trees and brush, pushing at the low branches with our bare hands so that they cut into our palms. I was sweaty, my shirt heavy against my clammy back.

Just as we were about to emerge into the clearing near the shore, Li pulled us to a stop. We peered out from the safety of the trees.

"Fifteen, maybe twenty paces to the beach," Li guessed. There would be no more protection from the trees. We'd have to cut across the clearing toward the shoreline and head south until we reached a spot where it'd be safe to enter the water. Otherwise, we risked cracking our heads open against the rocks. We quickly stripped down to our briefs, leaving our clothes hidden away under a rock beneath a tree.

We both fell silent, listening hard. I expected to hear barking, dogs coming straight for us. But all was quiet. This was our chance. The guards would be on opposite sides of the beach right now, which gave us the biggest window of time to get into the water without being spotted.

I braced myself, ready to tear across to the sand, but Li reached out to stop me.

I thought he had changed his mind, that he was calling it off. But instead, he gave me a weak smile.

"Good luck, brother." His fingers dug into my arm.

I smiled back. This former Red Guard, a city slicker who had once proudly touted quotes from Mao, truly was like a brother to me now. We were one and the same. And I recalled the old quote from my father. *It doesn't matter where they're from—all desperate men are the same.*

Finally, Li released his grip, and I felt the blood rush into my arm again.

And then he was off.

My feet felt detached from the rest of me. It was hard to keep up with Li's long strides, and I lagged several paces behind. I could hear Li panting as he pumped his arms and legs, all the while scanning the beach for flashlights and guards.

We veered to the left, following the coastline toward the beach. The ground was all rocks and short grass, but now all I could hear was the crashing of waves ahead. By the sound of them, I imagined them to be several yards high, but when I looked out, they were half my height at most.

The beach came into view, and Li glanced over his shoulder and broke into a huge smile. The ground beneath our feet was giving way to coarse sand. We were sprinting now, the water calling out to us. It seemed like a triumph just to have made it here, even though there was still the long journey ahead.

"Sei laa!" Li stopped short and pointed ahead. At the other end of the beach, I could just make out the silhouette of a guard and his dog. We had misjudged their movements, but there was no point in going back.

The guard's torch was pointed away from us, and I knew we had to act quickly. He hadn't spotted us, and we waded into the surf. It was cool but not unforgiving. The waves lapped at our toes, pulling us gently in.

I couldn't stop smiling. It felt like the pull of destiny.

Li paused for just a second. He should have looked ridiculous with his underwear billowing around his legs after all the weight he'd lost. It reminded me of that first night we'd gone swimming. The wind blew his hair back, and he stretched his arms out like a gull. Gazing serenely out to sea, he looked majestic.

As we slipped into the ocean, a cry came in the distance. We'd been spotted. But the barking of the dog and the yells of the guard were drowned out by the rushing of the waves. My tears of joy and loss melted into the salty water. And we began to swim.

★ ★ ★

Stroke, stroke, kick, kick, stroke, stroke, kick, kick.

I pushed through the water, straining to keep my arms and legs from breaking the surface as I paddled hard. Any splashing would have been a dead giveaway, so I kept my limbs churning underwater like the dogs did. My lungs already felt raw. I was burning energy too fast and not moving forward quickly enough. Still I kept up the halting rhythm.

Stroke, stroke, kick, kick, stroke, stroke, kick, kick.

I was aware of nothing but the black, black sea. The rocky beach had long disappeared behind me. The inky water pushed against my chest and wrapped around the numbness of my limbs.

Stroke, stroke, kick, kick, stroke, stroke, kick, kick.

The waves beat against me, a gentle lulling and wet slapping. I was feeling warmer now, and my breathing was starting to calm down.

Stroke, kick. Stroke, kick. Stroke, kick.

I switched to a clumsy breaststroke, my head ducking beneath the surface. I'd heard a saying once—the more time you spent with your head submerged, the more likely you would find the breath of the fishes. But it was also tiring to hold my neck up.

Stroke, stroke, kick, kick, stroke, stroke, kick, kick.

My limbs were tiring, pulling, pushing—completely numb. I squinted at a shape in the distance. It was still at first, an innocuous shadow, but then it quickly ducked beneath the waves.

Panic gripped me as my mind raced through the possibilities of what could be in the water with me. I wanted to call Li's name, but my lips were sealed by salt water. *Was that splashing?* But I couldn't see a thing.

I heard the distinct rumbling of a motorboat, getting louder by the moment. My muscles seized, and fear lashed through me, but then I saw that it was headed in the other direction. There was shouting, and I could see silhouettes pointing from the vessel. I dunked my head, pushing my limbs out and through the water, kicking beneath the surface. I changed course to give the boat a wide berth. Finally, when my lungs screamed for air, I surfaced, staying as silent as I could.

No light shone in my direction; no shouts came, telling me to stop. Once again, I was surrounded by nothing but the blackness. The boat and whatever it was following had vanished.

Nothing to do now but keep swimming.

Stroke, kick. Stroke, kick. Stroke, kick.

I paddled endlessly, trying to think of anything but the straining of my muscles.

I thought of my father. I imagined his long body pushing against the current and mimicked his strokes. I could see his head bobbing up and back under the water, following the distant light that would lead him to his new life. A new beginning.

I wasn't sure how long I swam like this, the image of my father and the strength of his dream spurring me on. It was as if his very spirit had entered my body, possessed it, his muscles moving me instead of my own.

And before I knew it, the island lay just ahead of me, close and real. We had made it. And I looked around for Li, but there was no sign of him. I knew better than to shout his name, so I whispered against the waves.

"Li."

There was no answer. I called again, keeping my head just above the water, my eyes peeled open for any splash or movement of a boy swimming for his life.

"Li."

And I realized I was alone.

The urge to turn back hit me hard, but I remembered the boat. I shook my head and tried to focus. The only thing I could do was keep pushing forward.

Stroke, kick. Stroke, kick. Stroke, kick.

That thin stretch of land loomed above me. I could just make out the cliffs and the sloping hills covered in trees. Dawn was about to break, and the silhouette was majestic against the slowly pinkening sky.

I paddled harder, though I had thought my arms and legs could give no more. It must have been close to two hours since we'd left the beach, but it was impossible to tell. All I knew now was the narrow sandbar I had spotted along the shore.

Stroke, kick. Stroke, kick. Stroke, kick.

It was teasing me, pulling away as I struggled against the surf. I knew I was close now, and I paddled even harder, calling on the tiny bit of strength I hadn't realized I still had. And then my feet hit the ground, and I collapsed on my hands and knees.

Crawling now, I pulled myself toward the beach. I imagined collapsing in a heap at this last moment. Drowning in a few inches of sea.

Finally, finally, I could stop. I lay there panting, my cheek against the sand, my face still submerged, salt water splashing against my teeth.

It was over.

I lay there until the sun rose and the sound of birds filled the morning air. Shoes crunched toward me.

A man in a khaki uniform peered down, his hands on his knees. He spoke with a clean, crisp accent.

"You sneaking in?"

I could barely nod.

He straightened up and peered up and down the beach.

"Only one of you?"

My tongue felt thick and limp, like it was not my own, and I struggled to find my voice.

"Yeah. Just me."

十八
CHAPTER 18

Hong Kong, British Dependent Territory

MING – 1973

Even after four years, Hong Kong still made me feel like I was melting into the ground. Every step I took, a little part of me was left behind, stuck to the pavement like sodden gum. While the village summers had certainly been hot and humid, it was nothing like the weather in this city. The heat of the pavement burned my skin, not to mention the constant crush of sweaty bodies pushing up against me. The towering steel and concrete buildings radiated like giant furnaces, so I felt like my insides were cooking when I stood underneath them.

This wasn't the paradise of freedom my father had spoken of. It was stifling and claustrophobic. Every day was a monotonous burden, and I was trapped.

After the official had found me on the beach, he'd called his colleague, who'd found a Hong Kong Police boat to take me to Kowloon. The guard escorting me had asked if I had any family here, and when I had mentioned Uncle Po, he'd grumbled under his breath so much that I thought he would toss me back into the harbor. But as it turned out, that was just his way. That was what I'd come to realize about Hong Kong officials and the police. Being a part of the government was a job, like working in a factory or out in the fields. There were some corrupt officials, no doubt about that, but there wasn't any of the political grandiosity that came with the Cadre title. Everyone was just doing their job.

The grumpy police officer had dropped me off in Kowloon, right on the Hong Kong harbor. I'd spent hours waiting there, wearing nothing but my holey briefs and wrapped in a towel the station provided. Once again, I was asked about family, distant relatives, anyone who could possibly look after me, claim responsibility for me in this strange land. I told them about Uncle Po, whom Ba was supposed to meet when he first arrived in Hong Kong. But when they pushed me further, I realized I didn't even know Uncle Po's first name.

Eventually, they did find a Po from Dingzai village living in the city. I spoke to him through a heavy piece of hard plastic that the police pressed to my ear. It was my first time using a telephone.

"Who's this?"

"It's . . . it's Ming. Ming Hong. I'm Ming Gwa's son."

"Ming Gwa? So gwaa? From Dapeng?" His voice was so loud that I had to lean away. I winced at the nickname he used for my father—*foolish melon.*

"Yeah . . . yeah. That's me."

"Aiyah! Last I heard, your father had died freedom swimming. What are you doing here?"

"Um." I eyed the officers nervously, but they seemed bored. "I came looking for you. I swam. I freedom swam."

Silence on the other end. I thought he would hear my heart beating through the phone.

He begrudgingly accepted me into his care and gave me a job at one of his factories for a pittance until I could work off my debt to him.

For the first six months, I didn't have a dime to call my own. The work was tough, sometimes even harder than being in the fields. Standing in the same spot every day for hours on end made my joints go stiff and ache from lack of use. My lean, taut muscles softened, and I was always dizzy from the lack of fresh air.

The hardest part about the city was the steady cacophony. All day, every day, the noise was never-ending: blaring, screeching, drilling, pounding, honking, yelling, hollering, cussing. And people rushed everywhere—to the bus, to the shops, to nowhere in particular. I had never known before arriving in Hong Kong that there was a particular sound for fast-moving people.

I lived with the other workers in the cramped factory dorms, more than twenty workers stuffed into a room about the size of the dorm back home. Every night, I went to sleep surrounded by the stench of sweat and body odor.

The other workers were friendly enough, but I mostly kept to myself. I hardly ever talked about Dapeng or about Tian or any of the other boys from back home. I hardly mentioned Ma or Ba except to say that they had both passed away and I was alone. And I never said a word about Fei, letting my burgeoning silence be the answer to everyone's curious questions about having a girl back home.

And most of all, I never, ever spoke of Li.

Over time, the memories of the village seemed to fade with the grind of Hong Kong life. The days and weeks blended into months, then years.

Once I was free of my debt, I spent every spare second working and saving money. I became obsessed with it, counting every cent, scrimping and saving every dollar I earned. Some of the other workers blew all their money on horse racing or women on their days off, but none of that appealed to me. *Time is money.* I had adopted this as my personal mantra.

I kept it in a secure pocket strapped to my chest that I took with me everywhere, even when I went for a bath. The bills were slowly accumulating so that the money belt made an unsightly bulge, despite the baggy clothes I tended to wear over my skinny frame. At night, with my ears still ringing from the din of the factory floor and pain shooting through the joints in my arms and fingers, I often found myself thinking about my father.

Was any of this a part of his dream?

★ ★ ★

I was strolling through the outskirts of Kowloon City one sticky evening. Summers in Hong Kong were worse than Dapeng; the soaring buildings and factory fumes meant there was nowhere for the mugginess to escape. I found myself wondering how things were back home, something I very rarely did. If I were there right now, I would be hunched over the stove, trying to coax it into flame so we could have our paltry evening meal. Would the city youths still be there? Would Feng and Commander Hongbing be gossiping and joking alongside Wang, Cho, and Tian?

My heart seized up, and I had to bat away the stinging at the corners of my eyes. This was why I rarely let myself think of home.

The sound of footsteps jolted me from my thoughts. They were close, more than one set of them. I rubbed my thumb against my shortened middle finger, a nervous habit I'd developed after I'd lost the tip of it in an accident in the factory.

I quickened my pace, but the footfalls followed. I counted three pairs of them now. Did I dare turn around? I cursed myself for wandering into an unfamiliar neighborhood, even if I had stuck to the main roads.

My pulse was racing, my eyes scanning the route ahead to see if I had a chance of losing them. But just as I came to the edge of a building, another figure emerged, blocking the way. He was short and stout, his mouth set midway between a grimace and a leer. There was a flash of steel—a sharp, thick butterfly knife was clutched in his left hand. I dared to look behind me; the others were closing in, clad in leather vests and thick hoodies, despite the heat. I was cornered like cattle. The boy in front of me was laughing, cackling like a demon. I wasn't sure how, but I'd ended up with my back against the wall.

"What have we got here? Huh?" The boy with the knife reached for my side, pointing the blade at my throat. "Grab him—we'll string him up by the balls."

Hands lunged forward, clutching my shirt and reaching underneath. I twisted and grunted, but I knew there was no point in crying out; no one would come to my aid.

"Wait, guys, stop." Out of nowhere, one of the boys in a thick hooded sweatshirt came forward, beating aside the arms and hands ready to pummel me. I slumped against the wall, but he yanked me up by the collar. I squinted, trying to make out his shadowy face under the dark hood.

He recognized me first.

"Ming. What the hell are you doing here?"

That voice was unmistakable, and he didn't need to throw back the hood for me to know exactly whose face was underneath.

It was Tian.

★ ★ ★

Daa Hyun Za. Big Circle Boys. That's what they called them-selves. Actually, it was what the Hong Kong Police called them—the criminal gangs of new immigrant youths from the Mainland, mostly from Guangzhou. Tian, of course, wasn't from the city. He'd come to Hong Kong about seven months ago, risking the swim across the bay the same way Li and I had four summers ago. He'd been taken to Kowloon, like I had, but instead of finding "family" like Uncle Po, Tian had struck out on his own. He'd tried a few factory jobs at first, then set up a hawker's cart, selling discarded fruit to unwitting tourists and passersby.

Eventually, the leader of the local Big Circle Boys had taken notice of Tian when he'd accidentally ventured onto their turf. He'd liked Tian's street smarts and stout build as well as his entrepreneurial character, so he had invited Tian to join the gang. The group was small and nimble, just fifteen strong, hardly the insurmountable number of the triads they often came across, like the 14K.

"Big Circle, see?" Tian grinned wide, proudly showing off the tattoo on his arm—a blackened circle with a thick ring around it, staring up at me like a lazy eye.

I didn't bother to mask my awe and reached out to touch it. The muscle was rock hard underneath the taut skin. "Wah. Hou ging." *Intense.* I wasn't sure if he was bordering on crazy or cool.

"It's like Guangzhou on a map, because it's a big city, see?" He had a new sort of know-it-all smugness about him. "I reckon the village wouldn't warrant a speck."

At the mention of home, we both grew somber. Tian lit up a

cigarette, an expensive Western brand that he would never have even seen in China, and exhaled a deep gray cloud.

"Ming, we thought you were dead. Why didn't you write to us?" His forehead was all pockmarked and sunken in, like a contoured map.

"I—I didn't think there was any need to. I didn't think you'd miss me." It sounded stupid, even to my own ears, but how could I explain the agony and pain of losing Li at sea? How Hong Kong had changed me?

Tian's face grew somber again, and he inhaled deeply. "Ming, you should have written. Even a line would have been nice. The way Li was going on—"

I shook my head. "Going on about what? Li's dead." Even after all this time, saying the words cut me open from the inside.

Tian blinked twice. "What do you mean? When did he die?"

I pinched my lips together and shut my eyes like I was willing myself to wake up from a dream. That way, I didn't have to say anything, and I wouldn't have to watch Tian's reaction. "He didn't make it. He didn't survive the swim."

I couldn't meet Tian's eye. He probably wouldn't really care, since I knew the two of them hadn't been that close, but I still didn't want him to see my shame.

"Ming." Tian's voice was surprisingly soft. "Li's alive. He made it back to the village. He said *you* were the one who drowned."

"Me? Drowned? But I called out for him. I looked for him, and he wasn't there. I was all by myself." I lost the ability to form sentences, thoughts, and phrases. Two words stood out.

Li's alive.

Li's alive.

Li wasn't dead.

I repeated this over and over in my mind, and eventually, my lips were moving too. "Li's not dead. Li's alive. Li's not dead." I was overwhelmed with glee and leapt to my feet, tossing my head back and grasping at my hair. "Li's alive. Li's not dead."

Tian smiled, patiently puffing at his cigarette, ever the gently mocking older brother. I was going to scream; I was going to skip out of the room and shout to the world.

Li was alive.

Finally, the shock and madness subsided, replaced by rapid-fire questions. "How, though? When I got to the island, he was gone. He had disappeared."

Tian scratched his head. "It was a shark. He was in bad shape; he said he almost bled out, but the guards from the patrol boat spotted him. It was lucky they did, because he had apparently passed out, so he was just bobbing there, and they almost didn't see him."

I remembered the boat, remembered holding my breath as I paddled past. The guards hadn't even glanced in my direction, keeping their torches trained on something in the distance. One had shouted at the other, and they'd sped off. Now I wondered if it was Li they had seen in the water. What would have happened if I had looked back instead of pushing on? "What happened?"

Tian stubbed out the rest of his cigarette. "He was cut pretty bad, so they had to take him to the big hospital in Tanshui to get patched up. He was there for a long while, and because of the severity of his crimes, no one was allowed to see him, not even his family.

"Afterward, when he was strong enough to leave the hospital, they sent him away. Labor camp, digging mud and firing bricks. All day, every day, he pushed wheelbarrows of dried mud to the kiln. He was only there for two years. Still, he was so skinny, so lean and brown, that when he finally came back to the village, no one recognized him."

"He came back to the village?" I was stunned. I'd have thought that after all that, he would have returned to the city to be with his mother and family.

"Yeah." Now Tian looked nervous, fumbling a bit as he lit another cigarette. I was ready to leap up, seize him by shoulders, but another part of me, the deep-down pit of me, filled with dread.

"Li came back to the village for a reason." Tian was stalling, flicking ash everywhere. "He was, ah—looking for someone. A friend."

I was confused. "Who was he looking for?"

Tian took a long drag, sucking all the courage out of that little burning stick. "Fei. He was looking for Fei."

I staggered and sank into my chair. The name was too familiar, and the memories gushed through me like the flood from a monsoon. I hadn't thought about her in a while, likely years, but now the sound of her voice, the touch of her skin, the smell of her crashed over me, one after the other.

There was a long silence. "She went back to the village?" I asked.

Tian nodded. "Not long after you left, Aunt Shu married a man from another village and took the boys with her. I guess that was why she was so desperate to see Fei go." He stubbed out the cigarette, only half smoked this time, and lit another.

"What about Fei's husband?"

"He was—well, I don't know, but this is what some of the villagers said about him—he wasn't all . . . *right*." Tian knitted his brow, racking his brain for what to say next. "They never had children. There were rumors that maybe he didn't prefer her *type*." And in typical Tian fashion, he mimed his intent, crooking his hands in front of his chest.

I choked on the air. Tian laughed awkwardly, then grew somber again.

"It was a while before she came back. She and Li wrote to each other when he was at the labor camp." He sighed. "Mostly, I think it was because they missed you. I just can't believe you're here. Why didn't you *write* to us?"

I was quiet again, at a loss for words. Li was alive. Fei was back in Long-chi. Nothing had changed. "Hongbing," I remembered suddenly. "And the other boys?"

Tian shook his head. "The commander was promoted and allowed to return to the city. That creepy brownnoser Feng married a girl from another village and moved there. The rest of them—Kamshui, Ah-Jun—they're still there. So is Wang. But Cho, he made the swim. He's just in Sham Shui Po. And when I heard he'd made it, I figured, why not?" Tian pressed his lips into a grim line. He let out a heavy sigh. "Ming, Ming. It's such a pity. I just wish you had let us know you'd made it. Everyone's going to be so surprised you're here."

I stood and wandered over to the tiny barred window. We were in Tian's apartment; he lived with two other Big Circle Boys. It was bigger than my cramped room, and they didn't even have to share a kitchen with other people; the life of a thug afforded some luxuries. The lights outside glared too brightly, the shape of them burning into my eyes. There were angry shouts and cussing from several stories below. This was the city Li and I had reached for. What would it have been like if he'd made it to shore? Would we still be friends? Living together, trying to make our fortune in the factories, more faceless Chinese workers in the congested chaos?

I closed my eyes, trying to imagine the little house that Ma and Ba had built. I tried to picture them in the hut, Ma preparing the family meal. But instead, all I could see was Li, his beautiful face twisted in frustration as he blew on the embers, coaxing them to their full dragon's breath. He broke into a smile when they finally caught, and somewhere I could hear a baby's laughter and a woman's voice calling his name.

"Ming, are you okay?" Tian's voice was full of worry.

Finally, I could speak. "It's okay. Let it stay that way."

"What are you talking about?"

"I mean, don't say anything about me. To Li or Fei or anyone back home." I turned to face him and used the most serious voice I could manage. "Just let them keep thinking I was lost at sea. That I never made it. Not a peep that you saw me, not to anyone. Not even Cho. Promise me you won't tell." My voice cracked then, betraying me a little, but I shook my head. "Promise me, Tian."

Tian nodded. And he stood and reached for me, always the big brother.

★ ★ ★

Tian took me out for noodles. We shared a cheap bowl of broth, and he told me about the gangster life while I recounted my time in the factory and showed him my shortened finger. Soon we were back to joking and laughing together, but a certain heaviness remained in the air. We weren't children anymore.

"So, what's with the pouch?" he asked, lighting up another cigarette.

I blushed, remembering our earlier encounter. "Is it really obvious?"

"Well, we didn't think you were pregnant." My face went redder, and Tian guffawed. Even after all this time, we had slipped right back into being brothers. The bottle of baijiu Tian had ordered was certainly helping.

"I . . . I'm saving money," I stammered. In Hong Kong, it felt like everyone had secrets but also that no one cared. But my humble village roots meant I was paranoid my intentions would be misconstrued.

"What for?"

"I want to move abroad. I want to move to America."

Tian leaned forward, squinting his eyes. "Are you drunk? How would the likes of you get a pass to America?"

I shook my head. "I heard there was a way; someone at the factory went. He found an immigration lawyer in the Walled City who helped him go to America."

Tian raised an eyebrow but said nothing.

★ ★ ★

I figured Tian had dismissed my admission as drunken talk, so I was surprised when he came to me a few days later.

"You were right, Ming." His eyes were wide and shining, a playful smirk on his lips.

"Right about what?"

"Going to America." He threw his arms up. "I asked my dai lo, and he says that he's heard about someone else who did it. He just needed a passport, answered a few questions, then paid a lawyer some money, and before you knew it, he was gone. In fact, I know where to find the lawyer."

My heart skipped. I couldn't believe my ears. "Do you—do you think you can introduce me?"

★ ★ ★

His name was Mr. Gee. Instead of the upper-class, British-sounding lawyers in those long white wigs in the Hong Kong movies, Mr. Gee was a bit rough around the edges. His hair was slicked back, and tattoos showed under his collar—a gangster in an ill-fitting suit. He worked for all the gangs in Hong Kong: 14K, Wo Shing Wo, and Tian's band of Big Circle Boys. Anyone with two cents to rub together was an immediate friend and dear client.

"So you left the Mainland four years ago? Freedom swimming?" Mr. Gee was sitting at a beat-up old desk in a cramped office, though it wasn't so much an office as a crumbling shed with tacky faux-leather furniture jammed into every corner.

"Y-ycah." I'd handed over a heap of grubby paperwork, nervously chewing on my lip, certain I'd filled out the pages incorrectly. The questions had been insanely complicated, using phrases and language I had never come across before—"current status not withstanding," "including any and all relations, past and present." If this was how city boys learned their letters, it was no wonder that Li had always sounded so eloquent.

"Hmmm." Mr. Gee ran his tongue along his top row of teeth,

showing off the gold cap that glittered up front. "The good news is that with all the ruckus that has been happening with Mao and the Communist Party in China, the U.S. government is now allowing more political refugees into the country from Hong Kong."

This was news to me—that even without any relations in America to help me and support my application, I could claim status as a refugee.

I hadn't considered that term before. I had accepted the term *new immigrant* and what that meant in the Hong Kong social hierarchy. But *refugee* was new.

Mr. Gee began asking me about my political ideas and lifestyle, how I had felt living under Communist rule. Even after all my time in Hong Kong, living in a "free society," I found myself struggling with my responses.

"What do you think of the Communist Party and Mao Zedong?" Mr. Gee asked me.

"They are the ruling Party of the People, and Mao is the Chairman and benevolent leader," I said straightaway.

Mr. Gee shook his head. "But do you think they are fair? That what they do is right?"

"I—I don't know." I had never once been asked this. None of the new immigrants or the Hong Kongese had ever asked me about the Party or this notion of fairness. As new immigrants, we all had our reasons for leaving, and the only thing that mattered was that we had survived.

Tian saw me struggling. "Big boss, what about the freedom swimming? Ming's a criminal now in the eyes of the Communist Party. It doesn't matter what he thinks about their leadership; he'd be arrested and tortured if he went back."

I winced, trying not to think of what Li had gone through when he'd been caught.

Mr. Gee mulled this over. "A boy who can't return to his country. Do you have family back home?"

I shook my head. "They . . . they died a while back." *Almost twelve years ago.*

The lawyer clicked his tongue, scribbling furiously. "So it is."

So I completed my application to enter America as a refugee. Even then, there was no guarantee that I would be accepted. Preference was given to people who were trying to reunite with their families in the U.S. and those with recognized professional skills, like doctors and lawyers. Refugees were at the bottom of the pile; we were the undesirables.

But I had hope.

And after nine months, it turned out hope was on my side.

★ ★ ★

The ship was enormous, a proper ocean liner that could have transported the entire population of Long-chi and more. I'd seen these ships traversing the harbor, looming over the tiny little fishing boats and junks, but until recently, I had never thought I would be boarding one, setting off to a distant foreign land.

That I would be leaving Hong Kong.

I reached into my jacket pocket again, feeling for the crisp sharp edge of my ticket and the crease of my approval papers. VALID FOR ONE-TIME ENTRY. I'd traced the lines of those English letters over and over until my fingers could draw them from memory.

"Relax. Anything you forgot, I'll look after for you." Tian gave me a wink. "Girlfriends too."

I had begged Tian to come with me, but he had refused, in typical Tian fashion. "I've got my eye on a girl. Or certain parts of her, anyway."

Said girl was hanging on to Tian's arm and playfully punched him for his lewd remark.

"Hey, remember to write this time," Tian chided. "I don't need to think you drowned again."

"Yeah, you going to learn how to read it?"

"You wish." He laughed and pulled me into a quick hug.

"Be careful, little brother. Take care," Tian said. His eyes were rimmed with tears. I felt a sob building up.

Tian, my first protector. My oldest friend. After all that we had shared, what could I say to him now?

I smiled and said the most inappropriate thing I could think of. "Sik si laa."

Tian cracked up, taken aback by my brashness. "Well, you're no longer the shy boy in the dorms." He hugged me again, this time long and hard, both of us holding on to each other because we couldn't bear to let go. We were true brothers, the kind who came together by choice, not by birth. And for us, the orphans, the fan ge ming undesirables, we were more family than we could ever have asked for.

And then, finally, I was on my way.

I joined the rest of the passengers out on the deck, waving goodbye to their loved ones gathered on the pier. I watched the sea of faces. Each one wore the same expression of loss and fear underneath the stiff polite mask of well-wishing and glee.

The blow of the horn drew our attention, calling us away from the port and our assembled memories as we were pulled out to sea. I stayed on deck, gazing out over the churning water.

I shut my eyes and imagined that instead of being up above the waves, I was down below, naked and kicking. I could hear Li's strokes beside me as we swam, our bodies moving swiftly, our hearts pushing us forward. I could feel the water all around us, soothing the fire that burned within as it brushed against our skin.

I opened my eyes, and I was still swimming. There were no lights this time to guide me, no beacon reaching out to me as I yearned for the promise of freedom. There was nothing but a vast expanse of ocean, brimming with potential.

And so I swam.

EPILOGUE

Guangzhou, Guangdong

LI – SPRING, 1977

The Cultural Revolution was officially over. Mao Zedong had died the previous September, and with his death, some of his long-standing policies were let go. Schools had been reopened, so Pearl was able to continue her studies. My brother, Tze, was due to marry a peasant girl from a nearby village.

And I was finally allowed to return home to Guangzhou with my young family.

It was New Year, and we were gathered in my mother's little apartment for the holidays. Ma looked so much older, her skin crinkled and ashen, and she walked with a stoop. "Aiyo, little Ming, watch out." Fei rushed to right the vase that had almost tipped over. Our son, Ming, remained oblivious, blowing spit bubbles and gurgling as he crawled around the room until his aunt Pearl scooped him up and gave him a big wet kiss.

Dinner was a feast for the eyes and the soul: dishes upon

dishes of the finest meats and seafood from across the province. With the end of the Cultural Revolution, we could enjoy such luxuries again, and no expense was spared. The smells mingled together over the tiny cramped table. We slurped and dug at delicious crab, enjoying one another's company. It was the first time our family had come together since I had been sent to Dingzai. And it was the first time we had done so without my father.

After dinner, my mother handed me a thin envelope. "I have a bit of mail for you and Fei. It's postmarked from overseas. From America. And registered too! What an expensive piece of mail." I cocked an eyebrow, curious. The only person I knew outside the Mainland was Tian in Hong Kong, and we only kept in touch via the rare postcard, since he couldn't read or write.

Pearl peered over my shoulder and made a grab for the envelope. "Wah! Look at all those stamps!"

But I kept it away from her. "Wah, Pearl," I teased. "Your future husband will be appalled at your childish antics."

She stuck out her tongue and went to help Ma in the kitchen.

Fei bounced Ming on her hip and gazed up at me. "Wow, who do you know from America, Li?" Her eyes were wide and wondering.

"Who do *we* know?" I traced the letters of both our names across the front of the envelope, trying to discover the secrets of their author.

And as I slid my fingers under the flap, the baby cooed.

AUTHOR'S NOTE

From the 1950s until 1974, thousands of Chinese youths braved shark-infested waters, not to mention severe punishment if they were captured, to make the grueling swim to the then-British colony of Hong Kong. They risked life and limb to escape famine, poverty, and political persecution in the hopes of having better lives and greater opportunity. Collectively, they were known in the media as freedom swimmers.

One of them was my father.

Freedom Swimmer is largely inspired by my father's story. Growing up, I knew very little about how he had come to America. Aside from telling us that he had lost both his parents and an older sister before he turned sixteen, my father was generally quiet about his past.

Writing this book gave me the chance not only to learn about my father's story but to understand more about this very significant and tumultuous time in Chinese history. I learned that he had survived not one but two famines that claimed so many lives, including those of his family. The experience has left me eternally grateful and amazingly humbled by the incredible lengths to which he and the other freedom swimmers went to find better lives.

ACKNOWLEDGMENTS

First and foremost, I have to thank my father, who was willing to relive the details of his past and spend tireless hours helping me over the phone out of fatherly love and devotion. And as much as this book is about my father, it would not have been remotely possible without my mother, who gave me the courage to write it and always offers her undying support for everything I do.

My eternal love and gratitude goes to Phil, my rock, my anchor, my keel, for keeping me steady throughout the process and reading my work through all its renditions and drafts.

Thanks to Tony and Barbara for being my early readers and for turning around their thoughts so quickly. Thanks also to David and the gorgeous members of my Spec Fic Writers Group—Kylie, Nat, Natasha, Ian, Mark, and Catherine—for reading and critiquing scenes and pages. Special appreciation goes to the Sydney Writers' Room for being the perfect space to work, and a shout-out to Kay and Bogs for keeping me sane and entertained.

And finally, all my gratitude and kudos to the team at Allen & Unwin and beyond. Anna McFarlane, for believing in me and seeing the potential of this book from the beginning; Brian

Cook, for your support; Jen Dougherty, for your incredible handling of run-on sentences and missing words; and the talented editorial and marketing teams behind it all. (An extra-special thank-you to Peter for the last-minute details at the end!) Your extraordinary efforts have made this book what it is. Thank you to the team at Scholastic for bringing this story to American shores.

ABOUT THE AUTHOR

Wai Chim was born in New York City. Although her parents didn't speak much English, Wai harbored a passion for books from a very young age, sneaking stories into bed to read well into the night. Wai graduated from Duke University with majors in economics and English. After graduation, she moved to Japan, where she spent over a year teaching English. She has lived in Sydney, Australia, for over fifteen years, enjoying the sun and pursuing her passion for writing. Wai is also the author of *The Surprising Power of a Good Dumpling*. To learn more, visit her online at waichim.com.